VERSES FOR HARRY

harry shapes fire and metal into truth
amanda walks beside him steady as tempered steel
geralt rises fierce when designs are stolen
a woman in shadow finds refuge
a circle of women lifts her toward a new horizon

HEATHER ANNE GORDON

This print edition published in 2025
by Centred in Choice

Sharing Australian voices, stories, strategies,
and skills with the world.

Title: Verses for Harry
Author: Heather Anne Gordon
verses written between 2020 and 2023 in Andamooka

First published by Centred in Choice
ABN 17 601 690 975

A catalogue record for this book is available from the National Library of Australia

ISBN 978-1-7635635-4-4
Author: Heather Anne Gordon
Title: Verses for Harry

We acknowledge and respect the deep spiritual connection and the relationship that First Nations people have to Country.

Country takes in everything within the landscape – landforms, waters, air, trees, rocks, plants, animals, foods, medicines, minerals, stories, and special places.

Connections to Country include cultural practices, knowledge, songs, stories, and art, as well as all people: past, present, and future.

Cover photographs: Heather Anne Gordon
metal roses sculpted by Ben Roberts, Andamooka
kettle on forge donated by Heather to Ben for shed tea

Internal Design: Karen Marree Engel

First Reader: Robyne Lesley

Dedicated to: Chado and Ben

Published by Centred in Choice
https://centredinchoice.com
PO Box 448 Alice Springs Northern Territory
0871 Australia

Heather Anne Gordon is an Australian artist, author, and children's book creator whose work moves with the rhythms of courage, creativity, and connection. Her stories breathe the scent of red dust and rain, carrying readers across landscapes where love, art, and resilience entwine.

Verses for Harry, a romance set in remote Australia, expands on characters from Desert Deluge, exploring the meeting point of steel and flame, solitude and desire, art and the quiet strength of survival.

Heather's creative practice flows between whimsical picture books and bold, experimental fiction, each shaped by her love of nature, community, and the quiet strength of everyday life.

When she isn't writing, Heather gathers fragments of paper, chocolate foils, colour, memory, building collages that reflect her stories: layered, luminous, and alive with possibility.

honouring

we honour the first artists
whose carvings and ochres
mapped sky and river and kin
whose weavings held stories
of rain and renewal
whose hands moved with memory
threading spirit through fibre
whose art was knowledge
law ceremony science love
and we remember always
art is not a frill
it is breath itself
it is how people remain
sane

when *desert deluge* was published
the words came back to me from readers
it needs more sex they said
i had written of weather of survival of bodies
against flood and drought
but they wanted the heat of desire the moans
the sweat the climax
and i carried that challenge quietly for years

could i write sex without shame
could i make the words explicit direct tender and raw
not hidden not softened not smoothed away
but real as the hiss of the torch the bend of steel

i thought of dictating the words aloud
how embarrassing if overheard
by the pastor next door
i thought of who to cast who could carry the fire
i circled always the question
what is it that is actually sexy

it is not only the mouth on skin the gasp of release
it is words themselves
words demanded words consented to
say it tell me what you want
the sound becomes touch
the language becomes tongue

so harry and amanda were born
two bodies welded into fire
two voices that did not flinch
chapters of lust tenderness work community art
sex not a distraction but a rhythm of survival

for sex has so often been used to shame women
to silence them to punish their hunger
and i remembered the words
of another south australian artist
who looked me up and down and said
if you cannot be outrageous now heather when can you be
and i held those words like flame in my hands

and i remembered too the voice of robyn archer ao
who said
"Art is not a frill on the frock of life, it is the very fabric:
without it we are naked to the often cruel, harsh and unjust
elements of life."
her words became my guide
because if art is fabric then sex is thread
woven through every life every story every body

so i wrote without apology
because art is everything
and sex is part of that everything
a way of knowing ourselves a way of being proud
a fire that will not be hidden
a fire that belongs in our stories without shame

Verses for Harry

part one

steamy sex and success

*they began as a fling
and became fire that reshaped steel
their story woven in sparks and skin
in community and in love*

part two

forging of courage and truth

*she began as silence unseen and unnamed
and became voice that claimed her own self
her story woven in courage and flight
in freedom and in fire of becoming whole*

contents

part one
steamy sex and success

they began as a fling
and became fire that reshaped steel
their story woven in sparks and skin
in community and in love

tinder dating

amanda walked in
fire already alive in her hazel eyes
curves soft but her step quick sharp full of energy
short brown hair
that refused to be anything but practical
her presence was a spark restless eager waiting for more

harry rose to meet her
tall broad the long dark beard showing a few grey hairs
his hi vis shirt smelling faintly of laundry detergent
long black hair pulled back with a bandanna
brown eyes steady olive skin weathered with work
the scars beneath the fabric unseen then
hidden histories pressed close under the work uniform

the heat begins with words
he whispers *i need your voice i need your say*
she trembles unsure if her mouth will obey
her silence a pause a playful delay
he presses his tongue slow
along skin just above lace
her hips shiver her hand seeks his face
she tries to push him lower tries to guide his head
he resists with a smile and a kiss instead
he says *words are fire words are flame*
there is nothing more seductive
than the naming of the name

her fingers tighten in his long hair
she pulls back his face
her voice breaks open her need takes space
i need you to lick me she breathes out raw
his tongue teases higher as if to withdraw
here he asks lips sliding up her belly
she moans little sounds warm wet jelly
no she gasps *lower still   my clit*
he strips the panties from her hips bit by bit
her swollen lips glisten exposed in the light
his eyes drink her in hungry with delight

just your clit he whispers *just the tip of my tongue*
she shakes her head *no all of it*
your fingers tongue lips use them all she cries
i need to come now no more delay
that was enough a command a gift
he buries his mouth deep her body will lift
she presses hard against him hair pulled tight
yes like this she moans as she rides the night
he licks slow circles drawing patterns clear
then faster then deeper heat burning near
up one side down the other he roams
her hips begin moving making his mouth home
her breath grows ragged her head tilts back
lost in the chase she rocks and she wracks

his hands grip her hips holding her down
as his tongue works steady her cries resound
sucking her clit pulling her into fire
she arches her back higher and higher
holy moly she gasps *do not stop   again*
he latches on tighter a relentless refrain
right there she screams a primal cry
her thighs shaking her body flying high
harry she calls his name like a song
her climax crashes sudden fierce and strong
fingers digging pulling his hair so wild
he tastes her fully messy beguiled
he keeps licking slower savouring sweet
while her moans unravel then fall to a slower breath

her chest heaves her cheeks burn red
hazel eyes sparkle wicked as she flops on the bed
he watches her glow still trembling inside
her legs still open her desire not denied
he smiles and waits for her breath to be slower
her body humming soft with afterglow
but she turns to him eyes alight with fire
if you do not have a condom you will earn my ire
her words a tease a promise a dare
a satisfied woman who still wants to share
and now the heat shifts the rhythm begins anew
her hand slides down his chest she knows what to do
her mouth remembers the taste of his skin
the length of his hunger the place she has been
she whispers *i want more* her lips at his ear
i want you inside me now i want you near

his breath catches heavy his pulse quick fast
he fumbles with foil the condom at last
rolling it down he feels her hand guide
her slick heat ready her legs open wide
the rhyme becomes rhythm their bodies aligned
a song of wet friction of hips intertwined
he thrusts she moans each push a wave
their cries entwined the sounds they crave
no format no rules just the pulse of consent
each movement a gift each moment well spent

she clenches around him urging him deep
he growls her name her body to keep
fingers tangled lips pressed hard
two lovers undone no need to guard
her back arches high her nails rasp his skin
the rhythm grows harder the world pulls in
his thrusts meet hers in furious heat
the slap of their flesh the pulse of the beat
she whispers harder he groans her name
each stroke fire each stroke flame
her thighs tremble her voice breaks free
come with me she gasps *come with me*
their bodies convulse their cries collide
the climax floods hot nothing to hide

they collapse together tangled in sweat
skin to skin breath to breath yet
the river of heat still hums still flows
desire not ended only slowed
she laughs low husky voice a tease
you are not done with me yet if you please
he kisses her mouth slow lingering taste
of her juices of heat of all they chased
their words return soft their touch not shy
love and lust twined no reason no why

the night is long the bed their sea
no structure no format only ecstasy
every lick every thrust every sound they make
becomes verse becomes rhyme a rhythm to take
consent their compass hunger their song
together they move all night long
for sex is not shame sex is not less
sex is the body's wild confession undress
s is for sex for sweat for sigh
for the earth of the body for the fire of the cry

the river does not end it bends it flows
through their limbs through the heat that grows
they ride it together harry and amanda
two bodies
one storm
one heat
under the verandah

the night has broken into dawn
sheets tangled bodies drawn
the room still smells of sweat and fire
her lips swollen her eyes still desire
she lies against him trembling unrestrained
he strokes her back slow each touch a refrain
no hurry no race the rhythm is slow
yet the warmth between them continues to glow

she whispers *you are trouble* her voice still husky
he laughs against her neck his beard rasping
she traces circles across his chest
small soft shapes where her fingers rest
last night she was wild fierce a flame
this morning she is tender yet the same
her gaze meets his steady and sure
their silence itself a sensual lure

he says *your words are what made me burn*
your words are what made the world turn
she bites his lip gentle teasing sweet
but last night i hardly had time to speak
he grins *then say it now tell me plain*
what you want again what drives you insane
her cheeks flush though the room is dim
she whispers *i want more i want you again*

he chuckles deep rolls her on top
their legs entangle her sigh a breath
of sound that lingers soft not rushed
yet still her thighs open brushed
by his fingers exploring slow
testing teasing letting go
she moans low but smiles too
last night was fire but morning is new

he kisses her mouth then down her breast
tongue circling nipple her body confessed
a shiver runs through she arches high
her laugh half moan half playful sigh
is this not routine she asks between gasps
you make me laugh as your mouth grasps
he says *routine no only flow*
last night was a fast river this morning is slow

their rhythm shifts softer but wet
her body still eager her heat now met
he slides inside her gentle sure
their eyes stay locked their trust secure
each thrust unhurried long and deep
like rocking to lull a child to sleep
yet still desire thickens again
their moans rising with the refrain

amanda cups his bearded face whispers his name
harry harry say mine the same
he breathes *amanda let yourself free*
together they move steady and strong
her nails press light her smile wide
their climax comes not fierce but tide
a wave that lifts then settles them still
their bodies joined their hearts filled

after they lie limbs loose in embrace
her hair spiky and wild across her face
he brushes it back kisses her brow
no words needed yet he speaks somehow
last night you were fire today you are flame
different shapes but the heat the same
she answers *i am both when i am free*
and you gave that freedom back to me

they drift to sleep again wrapped tight
the morning sun now clear and bright
their laughter returns when they wake once more
she steals his shirt and heads for the door
coffee she says *i will make it strong*
he watches her walk hums a song
no shame no doubt no need to pretend
their night their morning a flow without end

harry was a man of routine
no matter how hot no matter how keen
each tinder night each fleeting embrace
ended with coffee prepared with grace
a travel mug set by the door
a kiss on the cheek nothing more
a hug polite no promises made
no lingering touch no plans to be laid
he would watch them leave hair still damp
from the shower or makeup smudged like a vamp
then return to bed stretch out wide
alone once more yet satisfied

but with amanda the air was strange
something subtle began to change
he rose as always slipped to the kitchen
his hands remembered each practiced mission
grind the beans pour the heat
fill the mug set it neat
but when he turned she was there
hair untamed skin bare
leaning in the doorway eyes amused
her voice low teasing but not confused
she said *you make coffee as if to send me away*
a gift for departure not a reason to stay
he froze with the to-go mug in his hand
this was not what he had planned

yet instead of fleeing instead of retreat
he found himself laughing his heart offbeat
he set the mug down returned to her side
her smile wide her body open her stride
she touched his chest kissed his cheek
said *i am not finished not yet this week*
he felt the ground shift beneath his feet
a rhythm broken a new one with promises sweet
they sat at the table mugs warm in their hands
no rushing no ending no tidy plans
they spoke of last night of laughter of fire
they spoke of her work of her secret desire
to be seen not as fleeting not as a name
on a list of lovers all the same

she wanted a river of water not a glass
she wanted the present not the past
and harry listening felt undone
for the first time his ritual was none
she did not leave at the hour he knew
she lingered long until morning grew
into afternoon sun heavy and slow
her laughter filling the room with glow
and when at last she rose to dress
she kissed him deep nothing less
no mug at the door no tidy end
but the start of a chapter where rules bend
harry who once thought routine was right
now longed for her touch in the coming night

the second night came not with planning but with pull
harry felt it all day her laugh something special
the way she had stayed long after the sun
the way she had undone what routine had done
his hands itched at memory his tongue recalled taste
his chest burned warm where her head had been placed
by evening he reached for his phone with a grin
not his pattern not his spin
usually he let silence stretch thin and wide
but with amanda he longed for her by his side

her reply was swift her words uncurled
you thought i would not want more of your world
i am still hungry she teased voice bold
come feed me again let the story unfold

he drove through the night the road alive
kangaroos goats sheep eyes yellow in the drive
headlights cut ribbons through dark desert air
each kilometre thudding a drumbeat there
the steering wheel hummed beneath his hands
as if it too knew desire's demands
dust rose behind him the stars kept still
the silence outside heavy with will

he remembered her laugh sudden and raw
her mouth daring his hunger her glance that saw
the truth of him rough edges and scars
a man not of tinder but of nights under stars
his pulse quickened body aware
this was no fling no illusion of air
his breath was a furnace his chest a drum
she had called and he had to come
when she opened the door her eyes wild in her face
the air shifted the night bent its space
her lips parting fire her skin flushed flame
time disappeared nothing remained the same

no wine no talk no careful lead
just mouths colliding bodies in need
she pressed him against the wall with a kiss
her hands impatient her tongue a hiss
he gasped and laughed her hunger raw
her nails down his back left burning awe
consent in every motion spoken aloud and sure
they stripped each other open nothing demure
she pushed him back onto the bed
crawled up his body as last night she had said
her folds wet her hips rolling slow
his hands gripped her waist guiding the flow

up and down she rode his length
moans spilling out in reckless strength
he thrust up meeting her pace
her hair whipping wild across her face
their rhythm grew frantic her cries sharp high
harry swore he would never deny
her body gripping tight her release near
she clutched his chest screamed clear
her climax shattered the air so bright
he followed her over into molten night

after they lay tangled breathless spent
his heart thudding his body bent
but instead of pulling away as before
she lay across him asked for more
tell me she whispered her lips at his ear
what it is you usually do when dawn is near
he smiled sheepish spoke his truth
how each lover left each ending smooth
how coffee was ritual a way to let go
no ties no talk just ebb and flow
she lifted her head eyes fierce wide
with me she said *you will not hide*

in that moment he knew she was right
the pattern broken the world alight
no to-go mug by the door no kiss goodbye
instead her laughter a lullaby
he pulled her close their sweat still wet
and whispered *amanda i am not done yet*
her answer a smile her hand a slide
down his chest once more the tide
rose again between them deep
their night became endless without sleep

the third night was not planned it was called
by a message from her that made his guard fall
you are not rid of me she texted bold clear
and his chest burned hot as if she were near

he arrived at her door not with flowers or wine
but with hunger and laughter both unrefined
they kissed in the hallway bodies already aware
of the fire between them the pull of the snare
yet when their clothes scattered across the floor
and their mouths found the heat they had tasted before
there was something new in the way they stayed
in the way their hands lingered not only played

after the frenzy after the cries
they lay together looking in eyes
and harry for once broke his rule
he spoke of his childhood of being the fool
who thought detachment was strength not pain
who learned routine as a way to contain

amanda listened her hand on his chest
her gaze unflinching her silence blessed
then she laughed soft her voice a balm
you are not the only one who learned to be calm
when inside was storm when need was fierce
i too made habits to soften the pierce

her words undressed him more than her hands
her honesty shaking the ground of his plans
he kissed her slow not lust but trust
and whispered *desire and love are both just*
two sides of freedom when given in full
when no one is pushed when no one is pulled

she smiled wicked yet soft as flame
you might not leave me the same
and he knew as he held her in bed
that routine was gone that the river had spread

no travel mug no neat goodbye
no polite hug no reason why
he brewed coffee in cups not to-go
and they drank it together watching the flow
of morning light spilling across her floor
and he knew he wanted more

their fourth night was laughter before heat
the air alive with teasing sweet
amanda tugged his shirt half off
and whispered slow *you are not enough*
he laughed against her skin teeth grazing her throat
not enough he said *i will take that on note*

she pushed him back hands on his chest
straddled his hips her smile confessed
that she was in charge that tonight was hers
she spoke with her eyes without needing words
her body rocked slow her breath in his ear
tell me she said *what is it you fear*
is it that i will stay is it that i will go
is it that you want me more than you show

he groaned beneath her the truth too near
his fingers dug deep holding the fear
i fear you he gasped *i fear the way*
you break my rules make me want you to stay
she pressed harder her hips a grind
his words unravelled his heart aligned
and when she lowered herself on his length
he gave in fully his last defence
spent

the sex was a game a contest of will
she teased and tormented slow until
he begged her harder begged her fast
her laugh was wicked her power vast
but when she let go when she rode him rough
he saw both the fire and the bluff
the woman who needed to be free
yet longed for more than a sexual spree

after they lay her hair damp on his chest
she whispered soft *what if i am best*
what if the others the mugs the door
were only rehearsals for something more
his throat was tight his breath unsteady
he kissed her hair said *maybe already*

the morning after he did not brew alone
she joined him in the kitchen as if her home
two mugs not one her laughter spilled
and he knew his walls had been drilled

harry woke before dawn as always
the habit of years pulling him from the sheets
his body still aching from her weight her grip her cries
but the rhythm of morning could not be denied

he slid from the bed careful not to wake her
pulled on boots heavy with toe caps of steel
his hands rough from grinding welding sparks
his mind already sketching shapes of sculpture
metal bent into curves as if they were her hips
steel welded into spirals like her hair on the pillow
art pulled from the fire
the same fire she stoked in him night after night

he lit the torch in the shed at the back of his house
blue flame sharp against cold air
sparks spat against metal
each strike another note
in a song he could not stop singing
obsessed his friends said
married to fire and steel they joked
but amanda had seen him in the glow
had touched his rough-blackened hands

and said
this too is sex
this too is creation
the way you bend steel until it yields to beauty
the way you burn
to make the world remember your shape

she stirred late that morning
padding barefoot through the kitchen
her job in an office left her desk-bound for hours
but she carried the fire of words in her voice
presentations sharp clients leaning in
her hazel eyes daring anyone to doubt her
she told him once she was tired of being polite
tired of meetings that swallowed her brilliance whole
but at night with him she could be feral
at dawn she could still be wild
with bed hair and no shoes
and he enjoyed her that way most of all

when she found him bent over his task
sweat shining at his temple
sparks dancing against the dawn
she leaned in the doorway her arms crossed
you said you had an early start she teased
i did he said without looking up
the steel was glowing orange in his grip
but so did you

that night their sex was slower but no less fierce
his hands still smelling of iron
her skin still smelling of soap
she tugged his hair whispered in his ear
make me your sculpture bend me until i break
and he did with reverence with hunger
with the patience of a man who knew creation took time
with the urgency of a man who feared losing her fire

afterwards she lay sprawled across his chest
her fingers tracing the burns and scars
that covered his body
each one a story each one a wound
she said *you give your body to the fire every day*
but you give your heart to me
do you even see the difference

he kissed her hair whispered *not anymore*
and for the first time he wondered
if the obsession that consumed him
might finally share its place with her

chapter eight

the mornings came earlier for harry than for her
the shed alive with sparks before the sun broke through
he bent steel into spirals into wings into shapes
that only his hands could imagine
only his torch could call true
each piece another confession
each piece another wound healed by fire

amanda watched sometimes from the doorway
her blouse half buttoned coffee in hand
her office job waiting spreadsheets meetings clients
but her eyes lingered not on her phone not on her watch
but on the curve of his shoulders the strength in his arms
she thought *he is most himself here*
and then smiled to know she had seen him
most bare in other ways too

at night she returned from her office tired
but his touch woke her again
she teased him for the burns on his forearms
the grease under his nails
said she would never let him near silk sheets
but she tugged him down into her cotton bed anyway
and when his rough hands traced fire along her skin
she moaned that steel and flesh were the same in him
both strong both soft both bent into beauty

their sex grew playful bold
sometimes she demanded
he treat her like one of his sculptures
bend me shape me hold me until i shine
sometimes he whispered *let me be undone in your hands*
and she did with wicked laughter with reverence too
their bodies a forge their bed a workbench
desire hammered heated quenched again and again

but something else grew in the pauses
in the mornings where he did not brew the travel mug
in the evenings where she stayed beyond midnight
in the way she laughed at his stubbornness
in the way he listened when she raged about her office
how men talked over her
how her brilliance was borrowed by others
he said *let me weld you a throne*
and she said *no build me a stage*
and they both laughed until the walls shook

yet beneath laughter was fear
for harry knew he had never stayed
never let routine break into permanence
and amanda had learned not to trust promises
words had failed her before
but still she came back
still she undressed him with her teeth with her honesty
still he woke before dawn aching for her body
and more dangerous aching for her voice

one night after sex their sweat still damp
her hair tangled across his chest
she whispered *i do not want to be*
just a sculpture you finish
i want to be the one you work on forever
and he pressed his lips into her hair
too raw to speak but his silence was already answer

harry was not a man who showed his work unfinished
the shed was his temple and fire his priest
each sculpture hidden until the metal was cooled
the welds ground smooth the form complete
to reveal them too early felt like stripping his own skin

but amanda's persistence was the same as her moans
relentless insistent fearless
she teased him between kisses
show me what you hide
show me what your hands burn for when i am not here
her voice the same that demanded his tongue
his cock his sweat
and in the dark his resistance broke

one night after sex when their bodies were slick
their laughter spilling through sheets
he rose naked pulled her by the hand
to the shed
lit only by the low hum of the beer fridge light
her eyes widened at the half-formed figures
steel bent but not yet beautiful
welds raw edges jagged
she ran her fingers along them fearless of splinters
and whispered *this is how you love*
not finished not polished
just hot and alive

he kissed her there pressed against iron
his tongue inside her mouth tasting her awe
her hand stroking his cock already hard again
he lifted her onto the workbench
her thighs open her back arched
the scent of steel and sweat mixing with her arousal
when he pushed into her she gasped
this is the real art she moaned
your cock my cunt the fire between us
his thrusts echoed like hammer strikes
her cries like sparks flying free

afterwards she laughed through panting breaths
hair stuck damp to her cheeks
you let me see what no one else has seen
and he knew she meant more than sculpture
he knew she meant himself

for days the thought stalked him
in the clang of his grinder
in the silence of her leaving for the office
love was not his design
he had welded steel into a thousand shapes
but he had never welded his life to another
and now he feared the strength of her fire
the danger of wanting her more than his torch
more than his morning ritual
more than the solitude that had always been his shield

amanda was not content with shadows
she had seen his shed in half-light
had felt steel beneath her thighs
but she wanted the ritual
the dawn discipline
the holy hour before the world woke

so one morning while the sky was still black
harry lit his torch sparks bursting like stars
and turned to find her in the doorway
wrapped in his hi-vis shirt
bare feet cold against the concrete floor
her hair messy from sleep her eyes bright
you think i cannot wake when you wake she teased
you think i cannot stand where you stand

he set down the torch his jaw tight
this was his time
his solitude
but she walked forward without fear
placed her hand safely above the steel
still warm still glowing
and whispered *show me how you bend it*

he laughed low
half annoyed half aroused
but her persistence was art in itself
so he lifted her hands
showed her how to hold
how to strike
how to listen for the hiss of flame meeting metal
she laughed when sparks flew wild
and he pulled her close against his chest
guiding her grip
his cock already hard pressing against her back

soon the welding mask was set aside
the torch quiet the steel cooling
and she was bent against the bench
panties pushed down her thighs spread wide
he entered her slow the heat of fire still on his skin
she moaned into the noise of the shed
each thrust echoing against corrugated iron walls
his hands on her hips her nails on the bench

sex and sculpture one rhythm
her body bent as metal bends
until she broke with a cry that filled the dawn
afterwards she sat on his lap
her breath ragged her cheeks flushed
she touched his face with dirty fingers
leaving streaks of soot on his jaw
you are obsessed she whispered
but so am i
and he knew she meant not only with steel
but with him

for nights he circled the thought like a fire
the sculpture incomplete restless in its frame
he watched the metal woman wait without soul
dreamed of a form that could breathe through steel
and when amanda spoke her fierce surrender
he felt the truth strike clean and certain
only her body could birth this shape
only her trust could bring the woman to life

she stood before him bare as breath
the forge heat trembling between them
her voice a whisper of daring and devotion
use me she said *let my body teach your hands*
let metal remember the curve of woman
make her strong from my yielding
so she will hold the fire as i have held you

he worked in silence the forge waiting
bandages dipped in wet white promise
the scent of plaster thick in the air
her skin gleaming under the slow setting light
each strip pressed smoothed shaped by his hands
her breath shallow as he mapped her form
every curve a memory caught in stillness
until she stood frozen a cocoon of herself
and he stepped back trembling with awe
to see her torso finally outlined in plaster

it builds as breath becomes belonging
the night of casting leaves no boundary unbroken
skin and steel both cooling in the dark
she moves through his shed
like memory made flesh
coffee and metal scent mingling at dawn
for the first time he lets her stay
through the sunrise through the grind of his tools
her laughter weaving with the sound of sparks
and he realises his mornings are no longer his alone
his obsession has grown new roots
her hands her fire her voice inside his

for the first time they speak without armour
not over shed beers where ideas drift and dissolve
but over enamel mugs of tea gone cool between them
the forge quiet the tools resting their breath
he says *maybe you should stay*
and she does not look away
the morning light spills over their silence
and something unnamed settles into being
two makers no longer pretending they are alone

for weeks they moved like flame and forge
his hands tracing the curve of plaster
her stillness holding breath against the torch
metal rings waiting to be welded
her torso rising from the frame
their labour a duet of heat and hunger

each night their sweat a sculpture
each morning her laughter tangled
in the hiss of steel and smoke
as sparks fell like small bright truths
they learned to shape endurance
to hammer love into form
to make art of the ache between them

but obsession has sharp edges
and solitude a hunger of its own
harry was a man built from routine
from the silence of dawn before words intruded
from the discipline of metal and fire
he needed the stillness like he needed breath

amanda was a woman of presence
her job a battlefield of voices
her brilliance pushed down by men in suits
her laughter too loud her ideas stolen
so when she came to him she wanted space
to be heard to be seen
to be more than a body writhing in his bed
she wanted to be the voice in his morning
the hand on his coffee cup
the fire that lit his torch

and so one morning
when she slipped into the shed
bare legs cold shirt loose around her hips
he did not smile as he had before
he frowned beneath his mask
said *not now*

and the words cut her like sparks to bare skin
she pulled the mask away her eyes fierce
not now she echoed
i gave you my nights my mornings my sweat
i bent with you i broke with you
and you think i will stand outside your shed
like a guest

he set down the torch anger sharp
this is my work this is my silence
without it i am nothing
she crossed her arms her voice unshaken
and with me you are everything
or do you not see that yet

the silence grew heavy
thicker than smoke thicker than sparks
they stared at one another
both breathing hard from a fight
not yet finished
both knowing they had already crossed a line
sex could be undone sweat could be forgotten
but truth once spoken welded itself to the air

he pulled her close then kissed her hard
anger turned to hunger
their clash became fire once more
her nails tore at his shirt his cock hard in her hand
he bent her against the steel bench
entered her rough and fast

their moans colliding with shouts with curses
each thrust an argument each cry an answer
until she came screaming his name
and he followed her body breaking against hers

afterwards they lay on the floor
concrete cold beneath them
sweat cooling in the dawn
her cheek pressed to his chest
his arms around her at last
he whispered raw and shaking
i have only ever trusted fire
but maybe you are fire too

she kissed his bearded jaw
her voice low
and maybe you are steel
but even steel bends for heat

the morning after the fight
the shed still smelled
of sex and smoke
sparks cooled into silence
the bench marked by sweat
harry woke with amanda sprawled across his chest
her hair a spiky mess her lips curved in sleep
and for the first time
he did not think of how to send her away

in the past there would have been a travel mug
coffee hot a kiss polite a hug by the door
routine polished into ritual
for every tinder date
a way to leave without weight without words
but amanda stirred and stretched
her eyes opening bright and unashamed
and she said *where is my to-go mug lover*
mocking him with a grin that melted his guard

he laughed hard the sound strange in his mouth
no mug he said *only this*
and he pulled her back against him kissed her slow
her laughter filled the air like sunlight breaking
and the fight of yesterday dissolved into warmth

later she wandered barefoot through his kitchen
wearing only his shirt
teasing him about the burns on his hands
the way he forgot to eat when he worked
the way he loved fire more than food
he watched her moving around his space
and something shifted inside him sharp as a spark
he thought *maybe this is what i have feared*
not her body not her fire but her staying

when she left that day it was not in a rush
no mug no routine no polite goodbye
she kissed him full lips lingering
her hand sliding across his chest as if claiming ground
and she said *see you tonight*
not a question not a test but a certainty
and he found himself nodding without hesitation

alone in the shed sparks flying once more
he welded curves that looked like her hips
a spiral that echoed her laugh
a flame that reminded him of her eyes
and when the steel hissed and cooled
he whispered her name into the smoke
and for the first time it did not feel like weakness
it felt like truth

amanda had seen his mornings sparks and steel
his sweat bending metal into shape
but now she wanted him to see her fire
the one that burned not in bed not in love
but in rooms filled with suits and screens

so one afternoon she texted him short and sharp
come pick me up at five
and though he hated the town and its glass windows
he found himself waiting outside
steel cap boots tapping against hard pavement

she appeared in heels and jacket
hair tied back lips painted dark
her stride quick her voice firm
a different woman
than the one who straddled him at night
a warrior with words instead of nails
her phone still buzzing as she stepped into his ute
she sighed long set it aside
and for the first time that day
softened against his shoulder

this is me she said
the me that fights for space fights to be heard
the me they want to silence but cannot
do you still want it

he grinned rough
i wanted you with your thighs around my head
i wanted you naked in my shed
and i still want this too

her laugh broke the tension her hand found his thigh
and when they drove away she leaned into him
heels kicked off jacket tossed in the back
she became amanda again
the one who tenderly stroked his burns
the one who moaned loud enough
to wake the kangaroos

that night in his bed she was restless
not from lack of orgasm
but from too much thought
she spoke of meetings where her voice was stolen
of ideas that became someone else's credit
her words a mix of rage and fatigue
he listened more than he spoke
his calloused hand tracing circles down her spine
and when her voice faltered
he kissed her shoulder
said *fuck them all*
let me weld you a crown you can wear into every room

she turned her head her eyes hot
i do not need a crown she said
i need a man who knows i am already queen
he smiled kissed her hard
and that night their sex was not a battle not a tease
but an offering slow and reverent
his mouth worshipping her
her body unfolding until she trembled with release
and whispered against his ear
you see me

in the morning
she was the first to brew the coffee
two mugs not one
her laughter bright in his kitchen
and harry realised he did not just want her in his bed
he wanted her in his mornings
in his nights
in the silence between sparks

the shed was where harry
welded his obsessions into form
but it was also where voices gathered
the smell of smoke
mixed with laughter and stories
for his friends came often
geralt chadowski and morgan fowler
and sometimes the aunties shirley sheila and pat
three sisters sharp with humour
and sharper with truth

amanda had only known the shed
as a place of sparks
a forge of heat and steel and sex
but one saturday night
harry pulled her by the hand
into the glow of firelight and voices
the tables scattered with beer bottles
playing cards and mugs of tea

geralt already leaning back in a chair
boots propped on a crate his laugh booming
morgan perched cross-legged on a bench
hair streaked with sunshine
her brown eyes alive with wit

and the aunties
seated like queens in folding chairs
passing biscuits around
as if it were sunday service

harry cleared his throat
awkward in the doorway
this is amanda he said
and for the first time his voice was shy
the shed went quiet for a breath
then shirley barked out *well about bloody time*
sheila clapped her hands with delight
pat raised her eyebrows in approval
and morgan leaned forward with a grin
if she can survive your welding fumes harry
she can survive anything

amanda laughed her nerves melting
she joined them
sat cross-legged on the floor
sipping beer as conversation sparked
around the shed

geralt and morgan
old colleagues from harry's police days
their stories still carrying the weight
of sirens and night shifts
banter polished by years of danger
and dark humour

the talk rolled on like a river
through memory and metal
geralt telling tales of jobs gone wrong
morgan sharp and clever cutting him down with wit
and harry
watching amanda's ease unfold
in their company
feeling the quiet shift of her belonging take root

the aunties reminiscing about harry as a boy
always with fire in his hands
always stubborn as iron
and now with someone willing to sit beside him

amanda spoke too of her work
her battles in glass towers
the room listened with respect
pat nodding fiercely
sheila muttering *men are the same everywhere*
morgan saying *you'll bend them like he bends steel*
and harry just sat back his chest swelling
pride and fear tangled in him
for never before had he let a woman sit here
never before had he allowed the shed
to be shared this way

the aunties had known harry as a baby
since he burned his fingers as a boy
trying to light matches in the shed
since he scowled when told *no*
since he grew into a man
who trusted fire more than people

shirley was the blunt one
sheila the soft one
pat the shrewd one with laughter tucked in her throat
together they had carried him through storms
together they guarded the stubborn man he had become

so when they met amanda they shared a look
a look women share
when they know more than they say
shirley leaned close to sheila
whispering loud enough to be heard
about bloody time
he brought home someone with fire in her
sheila nodded eyes warm
pat only smiled her secret smile
and harry groaned because he knew what it meant
the aunties had already decided
and once they decided nothing could undo it

amanda did not shrink under their gaze
she laughed when shirley teased her
she matched wit for wit with pat
she responded gently when sheila asked about her family
and when she spoke of her battles at work
of meeting rooms where men borrowed her words
the aunties hummed their disapproval
like a chorus of magpies defending their nest
girl you keep talking pat said
because men only win when we go quiet

after that night the aunties began to plot
little things at first
dropping hints about sunday roasts
sending harry home with leftovers enough for two
casually mentioning amanda's name in town
as if she were already stitched into the quilt

harry noticed and felt the ground shift
he had lived long with solitude
routine like armour
but now everyone around him seemed to conspire
to keep her in his shed in his mornings in his life

geralt teased him openly
mate you finally found
someone who can weld your mouth shut
morgan smirked said
about time you stopped brooding in sparks

and the aunties smiled behind their teacups
pretending innocence but glowing with delight
amanda only laughed
her eyes sparkling when she caught their scheming
she leaned close to harry one night
as they sat on the bench with sparks dying low
and whispered *you know they have already claimed me*
his throat tightened but he kissed her hair
and whispered back *maybe i have too*

then the aunties
picked up their winnings from the card game
coins and notes folded neat into worn purses
their laughter soft as the night thinned
when geralt and morgan
finally staggered out still laughing
voices fading down the gravel track
the aunties waved their goodbyes from the doorway
leaving a faint fragrance of triumph behind

and in the hush that followed
amanda stayed behind with harry
the forge light low
the air thick with something new
neither work nor friendship but the edge of both
the sparks dim the silence warm
she whispered *i think i love your people*
and he kissed her slow
whispered back *they are my fire too*
but you are the flame i never thought would stay

harry had always built shapes of flame and shadow
twisted metal bent into curves
abstract pieces that spoke only to him
steel arms reaching skyward
scrap folded into sorrow and strength
but never a body never a face

until amanda

he found himself pulling from piles of rust
discarded steel old car doors broken pipes
the raw material had not changed
but his hunger had
his torch hissed alive
and he began to weld a woman

not soft not fragile
but tall as life
a warrior born from fire
her shoulders broad her chest proud
hands outstretched not for battle alone
but for care for gathering for holding
each plate hammered into muscle
each seam smoothed into form
until the sculpture rose fierce and tender both

his friends gathered one night to watch it take shape
geralt whistling low
morgan muttering *you have finally gone mad*
but the aunties only smiled deviously
pat whispering to shirley
look at him building her twice

amanda stood silent at first
eyes wide watching the figure grow from sparks
and when harry stepped back sweat dripping
mask lifted breath ragged
he asked *well*
his voice sharp with fear

she stepped forward
placed her palm against the cold steel breast
and whispered *this is me*
not how i look but how i fight how i love
you see me in metal

he exhaled a sound between laugh and groan
because it was true
her body was heat her voice was blade
her care was shield her sex was fire
and now the shed held her not only in memory
but in iron

that night they fucked against the sculpture
her back pressed to steel her moans echoing
she laughed between gasps
so this is what it means to be immortal
and he whispered *yes*
burning inside her as if to weld them together

in the morning she traced the seams
steel cool beneath her fingers
and said *you built a woman who fights and cares*
but i am already her
you only had to notice

he kissed her hair whispered
i notice now

the day came
when harry could no longer keep her hidden
the warrior woman stood tall in the shed
her steel shoulders gleaming her arms outstretched
a monument to fire and love and fight

geralt and morgan arrived first
geralt whistling long and low
mate you have lost your bloody mind he said
but his grin was wide his eyes bright
morgan folded her arms
so the man who never welded faces never welded hearts
has built a woman taller than himself
about time your art stopped sulking

then the aunties came
shirley with biscuits in hand
sheila with a thermos of tea
pat with her pack of cards and crafty smile
they circled the figure slow   their chatter sharp as birds
look at her shirley said
a woman with no fear in her stance
a woman who will outlive him
sheila touched the cold steel hand
this is care made visible she murmured
and pat only smirked and repeated
about bloody time

amanda stood quiet through it all
her face unreadable until the room softened
then she stepped forward
placed her hand on the warrior's chest
her voice low but clear
this is me and not me
this is every woman who fights
every woman who loves anyway
harry built her from scrap
but he built her from knowing me

the shed went silent
sparks sizzled in the corner
and harry for once did not look away
he met their eyes all of them
his friends his aunties amanda
and let them see him bare

that night when the visitors had gone
the shed still humming with ghosts of laughter
harry sat on the bench shoulders heavy
and amanda climbed onto his lap
kissed him deep until he tasted her smile
she whispered *you built love from rust*
and he whispered back
maybe love was always waiting in the scrap

chapter eighteen

amanda found him again in the shed
sparks rising like impatient stars
the smell of steel and sweat pressed heavy in the air
he was bent over the figure
grinding welding shaping
the warrior woman already breathing in her silence
but harry's eyes were weary
his hands roughened not only by work but by doubt

he muttered *she is not ready*
she is only scrap only a shadow
no one will want her
not for the seaside not for the show
i am just a man hiding in a shed
what do i know of art

amanda stepped closer
her camera swinging against her hip
her eyes sharper than his torch
you know more than you think harry
this woman is more than steel
she is the story you could never say
the grief the fire the fight
all welded into form

she lifted the camera and clicked
each frame a fragment of truth
the curve of a shoulder
the burn of flame marks
the hands that shaped her
the silence that filled the shed

harry turned away muttering again
they will laugh at me
they will laugh at her
i cannot stand before them

but amanda placed the photographs in his hands
black and white lines stark against his dirt
see she said
see how she already commands the room
see how she stands stronger than both of us
this is not only sculpture harry
this is statement
this is survival
this is a woman forged from nothing and refusing to fall

she sat at the old desk in the corner
pulled paper towards her
began to write
with the same rhythm she wrote her own name
artist statement she scrawled
her words flowing like sparks

the warrior woman stands for resilience
for care for fire for those who refuse to be bent
a form of steel holding both love and rage
a body that remembers touch
a body that defies silence

harry stopped working
listened
each word of hers
like a hand lifting him from doubt
but still he said softly
i cannot submit it
i do not belong with those who stand in white shirts
who drink wine and talk clever

amanda laughed low and sure
you belong where your fire burns
and your fire has burned her into being
you only need to let her breathe
i will send the photographs
i will send the words
you will not have to stand before them
not yet
but your warrior will

harry looked at her then
really looked
and saw how she too was warrior
camera slung like a weapon
words cutting deeper than flame
and for the first time he nodded
a small nod heavy with surrender

so the entry was sent
the warrior woman carried in envelopes of image and ink
out of the shed into the world
word travelled faster than they expected
geralt booming through the pub
reckon our harry is finally taking his fire out of hiding
morgan shaking her head smiling that crooked smile
her cleft chin accentuating her happy grin
the aunties busying themselves
with biscuits and opinions
shirley declaring she will wear her brightest shirt
sheila insisting the good spaces will be taken
if they do not arrive early
pat saying little this time but listening to everything

harry sat trembling in the shed
hearing the murmurs gather like surf at night
and amanda held his hand
telling him again and again
she is ready harry
and so are you

the day of the exhibition
the sky was wide with salt and light
waves rolling heavy against the sand
brighton jetty stretching out like a finger into the gulf
children running
with ice cream dripping down their wrists
couples walking hand in hand

and there beside a seat overlooking the sea
stood the warrior woman of steel
harry's hands all over her form
his sweat his fire his nights of obsession
her shoulders proud her chest open
her arms outstretched not to fight but to hold
her skin burnished by flame marks that glowed in the sun

the crowd gathered curious at first
tourists pausing locals murmuring
geralt with his booming laugh saying
mate you finally brought the shed into daylight
morgan shaking her head with a smile
the aunties dressed in their best
shirley announcing loudly
look at our harry building a woman
worth more than the words of any man
sheila dabbing her eyes
pat smirking secret as always

but it was amanda who drew the whispers
amanda whose presence burned brighter than sparks
because everyone could see what she already knew
this warrior woman was her
not her face not her exact frame
but her fight her care her fire
and the way harry looked at her
standing beside the sculpture
was the unveiling of a heart as much as art

when the mayor praised through a speech
calling it a triumph of recycled beauty
harry barely heard
he stood stiff his hands filthy still with grit
his boots out of place on the promenade
until amanda slipped her hand into his
her grip steady her smile wicked and soft
and he breathed again

after the ribbon was cut after photos were taken
children climbing into the sculpture's outstretched arms
other women touching the cold metal with reverence
harry and amanda sat together on the seat
the warrior towering beside them
waves breaking like applause below
the aunties circling with gossip and biscuits
geralt and morgan
already arguing over which bar to celebrate in

and amanda leaned close to whisper in his ear
you built me from scrap
and you placed me here where the world can see
but what you do not know harry
is that you also built yourself
because only a man ready to love
could have made her

he turned his head kissed her slow
not caring who watched
and the warrior woman gleamed in the sunlight
a witness to their fire
a promise welded into steel and sea

chapter twenty

the warrior woman stood gleaming by the sea
her arms open her body strong
children climbed her shoulders lovers
leaned against her
tourists snapped photos at sunset
and the council printed flyers
calling her a triumph of recycled art

harry did not go to see the next day
not after the unveiling
not after the speeches and claps
he returned to the shed
to sparks and steel where silence still obeyed him
but the world followed him in
reporters calling
art critics writing his name
the phone ringing with offers commissions interviews

he felt stripped bare
exposed in ways sparks had never done
because every word they wrote every praise they gave
was not about him alone
it was about her

at night amanda found him restless
sitting on the shed bench head in his hands
he muttered *i do not deserve this*
they do not know the truth
they do not know that it was you
your fire your fight your voice in my blood
without you i would still be welding shadows
without you i would never have built her

she sat beside him slid her arm across his shoulders
and said *harry you do not understand*
this was never about me alone
the steel was yours the fire was yours
you gave her form i only gave you reason
do not tell me you are not deserving
because deserving is not the point
the point is she exists
and the world needed her

he shook his head rough
the applause feels like theft
their words are not for me
they are for the woman who broke me open

her laughter cut the silence warm and sharp
then let them be for both of us
let them see what happens when fire meets fire
when steel bends not to break but to love

and she kissed him hard
until the weight of recognition melted into sweat
until his doubt became moans against her skin
until they both remembered that glory was nothing
compared to the heat of her thighs around him

later lying tangled in sheets
she whispered *i will take your guilt*
if you will take my pride
and for the first time he thought maybe
recognition was not something to fear
if it meant she was standing beside him in the light

the calls kept coming
art festivals councils galleries wanting his name
the man who welded a warrior from scrap
the welder who bent steel into love

harry had never been a man of contracts
his youth a knot of trouble
his badge once polished now taken back by injury
life measured not in dreams but in shifts
pay slips folded into envelopes neat numbers lined up
steady steady he told himself
the welding had begun as rehabilitation
hands relearning patience through flame and steel
it grew into the permanent job at the boiler shop
heat searing metal skin hot sparks burning air
dangerous yes but predictable
steady safe steady safe steady safe
until now when even the plodding future
the slow creation of essentials for the mining industry
and regular pay
seemed at risk

now the shed felt different
each spark not just art but livelihood
each sculpture a risk each commission a chance
and the old job waiting behind him like a shadow
you can always come back the foreman said
but harry knew he could not
not after sculptures by the sea
not after the warrior woman

at night he lay restless beside amanda
her skin warm her breathing steady
while doubt burned his gut raw
what if the phone stops ringing
what if no one wants another sculpture
what if the bills stack high
what if i let her down

he whispered this one night
voice rough in the dark
and she rolled onto her side
eyes sharp even in shadow
you think i wanted you for your pay slip she said
you think i opened my legs for your shift work
you think my heart moans
when i hear the sound of a time clock
no harry
i wanted you because you burn
because you create what no one else can
because you made me in steel and showed me to the world

he groaned low pressed his face to her chest
said *but the numbers the rent the bloody groceries*
and she laughed her husky laugh
then we live smaller then we hustle then we fight
you are not alone anymore
i know how to fight too

he kissed her there
his doubt tangled with her certainty
and when they fucked that night
it was not for escape
but for survival
each thrust a vow each moan a promise
that they would build not just steel not just art
but a life raw and risky and free

in the morning he brewed coffee slow
two mugs side by side no travel lid in sight
he watched her sip hers eyes gleaming over the rim
and thought *if she stays*
maybe i can risk everything

the first commission after the sculptures
came from a council inland
they wanted strength made visible
they wanted a sculpture that spoke of resilience
and the cheque was larger than anything
harry had seen from sparks before

he stared at the numbers his hands shaking
the paper smudged with sweat
he could feel the pull of the old job behind him
the steady wage the safe routine
and the wild new river before him
uncertain uncharted but alive with fire

that night he told amanda
his voice low heavy with fear
if i take this on i leave the boiler shop for good
i bet it all on steel
i bet it all on you

she turned her head sharply her eyes bright
on me she asked
you think this is about me
you think i am the reason you weld you burn
you were fire before i walked into your shed harry
you made sparks
long before my thighs wrapped around you

he groaned rubbed his temples
but the warrior was you
sculptures by the sea was you
every shape i see now is you

she softened then
touched his face with a hand gentle and fierce
maybe i lit the match she said
but you carried the torch your whole life
do not give me all the blame or all the credit
love is not a bet harry
love is the steel you already hold
it bends but does not break

he wanted to believe her
but in the dark the doubts whispered loud
what if she left
what if the fire dimmed
what if he gave up certainty
for a woman who could one day walk away

later when she climbed onto him
her mouth hot on his chest
her hands firm on his shoulders
he thought *maybe this is worth every risk*
maybe even if she goes the fire she gave me will stay

and as she rode him until they both cried out
sweat slick and laughter tangled
he realised the truth was simple
he was not betting it all on her
he was betting it all on himself at last
and she was choosing to stand in the fire with him

the contract signed heavy with ink
the council's deposit slip tucked into his pocket
harry felt the ground shift beneath his boots
he was no longer just a welder at the boiler shop
he was an artist on his own
and the weight of it pressed harder than steel

he began the build in the shed
sheets of scrap bent under his torch
sparks flying like birds across the night
each strike of the hammer an echo of doubt
what if it fails
what if they laugh
what if the money runs out before the sculpture stands

amanda was there most evenings
heels kicked off jacket tossed across a chair
her office day discarded as she stepped into his world
she cheered him when sparks burned high
she teased him when he scowled too long at the frame
she pressed herself against him at the bench
and whispered into his ear
you cannot lose yourself to fear
because if you do you will lose me too

her voice was both balm and blade
when he snapped she snapped sharper
when he sulked she laughed until he cracked
when he doubted she reminded him
you chose this not for me not for them
but for the fire that already lived in your bones
and when he tried to give her credit for everything
she pressed her palm against his chest
and said *no harry you made her real*
i only made you believe you could

their nights remained wild
sheets soaked bodies tangled
but even in bed she did not let him off easy
one night riding him slow
her voice steady through her moans
she said *you are not just fucking me harry*
you are fucking your own fear
and he came with her name on his lips
realising she was right

weeks turned into months
the sculpture rose higher
a shape of defiance and grace
the community already whispering

the boss at the boiler shop was already asking
when he would return work was steady again
and good men were hard to find
harry missed the camaraderie
the clang of steel and the clang of laughter
those crude jokes that filled the gaps between welds
when someone said *a hot rod fills the gap*
and the others sighed with laughter
as a full penetration butt weld
was laid clean and true
they had language there
born of heat and sparks and sweat
banter that masked exhaustion
and pride hidden under grime

yet now the shed held a different hum
the slow shaping of steel into stories
the hiss of flame a meditation
the silence almost sacred
and he wondered if creation
was just another kind of welding
joining what was once separate
and holding fast against time
and harry standing in sweat and sparks
looked at the half-formed metal figure
and thought of amanda's words
love is not a bet
steel bends but does not break
for the first time he believed it might be true

the sculpture neared completion
steel seams smoothed sparks cooled into curves
the figure rose tall proud resilient
and each day harry felt the knot in his chest tighten
for he had to show her
and that felt harder than the torch
harder than the hammer
he had built the warrior
for the sculpture exhibition
for the world
but this commission this figure
was not for the council not for the papers
it was for amanda first
and he feared
the way her eyes could strip him bare
more than he feared critics or crowds
for nights he delayed
working late telling her *not yet*
claiming details unfinished angles not right
but she knew the truth
she saw the way his jaw clenched
the way his shoulders sagged when she entered the shed
and one evening she called him out
harry you can strip me naked in front of sparks
you can make me scream on your workbench
but you cannot show me what you built with your hands
what are you so afraid of

his torch hissed quiet
he set it down his voice rough
that you will not see yourself in her
that you will think i failed you

her laughter was not cruel but soft
she cupped his face smudging grease on his cheeks
harry i never asked you to weld me
i asked you to weld truth
and truth is not failure

he swallowed hard then led her to the figure
covered with a tarp heavy with dust
his heart hammering like steel struck
and when he pulled it away
the warrior stood revealed
not amanda's body not her exact face
but the shape of her fight the curve of her care
arms outstretched like shield and embrace

silence fell
only the hum of night air
only the faint creak of metal cooling
he stared at her face waiting for disappointment
but amanda's eyes filled with tears
she stepped forward touched the steel hand
and whispered *this is not me alone*
this is every woman who has ever held too much
who has ever fought and still loved

she turned to him then
kissed him deep
fierce until sparks reignited between them
and against the half-finished sculpture
she pressed her body to his
whispered in his ear
do you see now
you did not fail me
you found me

and when they made love
there in the glow of cooling steel
it was not only lust not only fire
but a surrender as frightening
and tender
as truth itself

the unveiling this time was inland
a dry square of earth ringed with gums
the council had chosen the site carefully
a place where resilience was needed
a place where drought and flood had bent people low

this warrior woman rose tall in the centre
steel gleaming under a fierce australian sun
arms out as if to gather the town into her chest
the crowd thick around her murmuring
farmers in work boots children tugging their sleeves
women pressing palms to the cold metal skin
as if drawing strength from her frame

harry stood apart
boots heavy throat tight
his name printed on banners
his work praised in speeches
but he heard only the hum of his doubts
i do not deserve this
i am a welder not a prophet
this was her this was always her

then he felt amanda's hand slip into his
her grip firm her gaze fierce
she leaned close so only he could hear
they are not only seeing me harry
they are seeing you
you carried fire into shape
you gave them a mirror they never knew they had
do not shrink now

the mayor murmured
through thanks and accolades
reporters snapped photographs
children clambered at the base of the sculpture
and still harry wanted to step back
until amanda pulled him forward
onto the small platform
where the microphones waited
she whispered *stand with me*
and when she spoke her voice carried like the wind

this is not just steel she said
this is us
this is every hand that works until calloused
every voice silenced until it rises
every woman who has fought and still cared
this is what resilience looks like
built from scraps but welded into strength

the crowd applauded with approval
and harry felt the wave of pride rise
fear tangled in it sharp and raw
but he stood still hand in hers
for the first time not hiding
for the first time allowing himself to be seen

that night when the town square was empty
they returned to the sculpture together
the steel still warm from sun
amanda pressed her body against his
kissed him slow beneath the warrior's shadow
and whispered *you cannot run from this harry*
this is who you are now
and he pressed his forehead to hers
and whispered *then i am yours as well*

the weeks after the unveiling were louder than he liked
newspapers printing his name
councils calling with offers
an exhibition in adelaide asking for submissions
and harry sat in his shed sweating
torch burning bright but his chest tight with doubt

he had always been fire and solitude
his only audience the hiss of steel
now the world wanted more
and with each request each spotlight
he felt something dangerous
that art might demand all of him
and love might slip away in the smoke

amanda was beside him still
heels kicked off jacket folded on the bench
her hair spiky her laugh sharp
she kissed him between sparks
teased him out of his brooding
but she saw the shadow gathering in his jaw
the way he looked at her as if she too
might one day be claimed by his work
instead of his hands

one night she climbed into his lap
straddling him fierce her voice low
you think i will let steel steal you from me
you think i will watch you weld yourself shut again
her words cut deeper than sparks
and his silence was answer enough
so she rode him hard
not playful not soft
but urgent like battle
her body demanding his body back from fear
her moans tearing through the shed walls
until he shouted her name raw and broken
until he remembered flesh over flame
until he collapsed gasping beneath her
and she whispered into his ear
you can have both harry
the art the love and the fire the steel
because i will not let you choose between them

afterwards as sweat cooled and silence settled
he touched her hair whispered
but what if the fire eats me
what if it eats us
she kissed his lips soft this time
then we feed it together she said
and it will never burn us hollow
and for the first time
he believed art and love might not destroy each other
but weld themselves into one

the invitation came with embossed lettering
an adelaide gallery asking him to exhibit
another warrior woman version
alongside more recent metal works
words like celebrated artist
and groundbreaking vision printed bold
harry held the envelope as if it might burn
his boots heavy against the shed floor

the shed had always been enough
sparks for audience steel for devotion
but now the city wanted to claim him
bright lights white walls
eyes he could not hide from

amanda read the letter over his shoulder
her lips curving into a grin
see she said
i told you the fire was bigger than this shed
but he only muttered low
i do not belong in a gallery
i belong here with torch and rust

she turned him by the chin
her voice sharp as blade
you belong wherever your art is
and your art is ready to be seen

so they went
him in a shirt too stiff for his liking
boots polished but still heavy
her in blue silk and red lips
walking beside him like flame incarnate
as if she had been born for rooms like these
the gallery was cold white light
wine glasses clinking
voices sharp with opinion
people circling the sculptures like vultures
praising angles seams shadows
as if they knew the sweat behind them

harry's pieces stood in quiet defiance
ammonites curled like memories of the deep
trilobite fossil dreams pressed into metal skin
roses twisted from rusted wire and tin
sturt desert peas blooming in welded flame
the colours of the desert reborn on car bonnets

critics murmured
words like composition and balance
their lips red with shiraz and self-importance
but amanda watched from the corner
saw not art but labour turned divine
the long nights of grind and fire
the soft murmur of his breath counting hammer blows
and she knew this was not display it was confession
the way a man speaks only through his hands

harry's chest ached his throat dry
until he felt her hand steady at his back
she whispered in his ear
stand tall they came for the fire you carry
not for the words they spin

when the curtain was pulled from the warrior
the crowd gasped the room hushed
and for a breath he hated it
the theft of silence the clatter of praise
until he saw her standing beside the steel figure
her eyes shining her pride unhidden
and he realised the unveiling was not theft
it was offering

the night wore long
reporters snapping questions
patrons circling wanting his card
but harry barely answered
he watched amanda
the way she defended him with sharp wit
the way she laughed at pretension
the way she pulled him into corners
kissed him quick when no one saw
her presence louder than the crowd
her body the only truth

later driving home down dark hills
her shoes off her head against the window
she whispered *you were fire in there*
even if you could not see it
and he reached for her hand rough and trembling
said *i only see it because you were there*

and in the silence of the ute
steel in the back rattling like bones
he wondered
if love itself was the truest exhibition

this success did not arrive gentle
it came like a flood bursting through the shed
letters offers requests all piling high
his name
suddenly worth more than his hours of sweat

harry tried to keep pace torch in hand
steel bending night after night
but the silence he once loved was gone
now every spark felt like a promise to strangers
every seam welded with expectation

amanda watched him wear thin
his eyes darker his shoulders tight
he kissed her distracted
touched her like a man still thinking of the welding flame
and though he still burned inside her
the rhythm was not theirs alone anymore
it carried the weight of the world's gaze

one evening she found him in the shed
mask tossed aside head in his hands
the sculpture behind him half-built half-forgotten
she crossed her arms leaned against the doorway
and said
you are fucking them more than you are fucking me

his head snapped up eyes raw
what are you talking about
she walked closer voice steady
you give them your hours your sweat your obsession
and you give me what is left over
but it was not them who made you burn again
it was us harry it was this shed this fire
do not lose what made you worthy of their praise
in the first place

he swallowed hard
his chest aching with truth
he wanted to argue wanted to defend
but her eyes cut him sharper than any blade
and he knew she was right

that night he laid his torch down
pulled her close with hands still blackened
and kissed her like he had the first time
rough full of need not performance
he carried her to the bench
lifted her onto it without a word
and when he thrust into her
it was not for release not for escape
but to reclaim the fire that belonged to them
moans rising louder than any crowd

afterwards she held his face
her voice soft but fierce
you do not have to choose harry
but you do have to remember
steel without love is just scrap
love without steel is just smoke
you are both

and for the first time he believed it again
that art and love did not compete
they welded
into something stronger than either alone

harry had always built alone
his shed his sanctuary
his torch his only companion
until amanda walked barefoot through its doors
until she pressed her fingers to raw metal
and whispered *you cannot keep me outside of this*

after the fight after the unveiling after the acclaim
he began to see the truth in her words
balance was not found in hiding her from the work
balance was forged by letting her in

so he laid out sketches rough lines on paper
something he had never shown another soul
figures half-drawn frames imagined
and she leaned over them hair brushing his arm
eyes sharp seeing what even he could not
this curve is wrong she said
this stance too heavy
and he bristled at first
until he saw her point
until he saw how her eye cut like his torch
and shaped the steel before it even bent

soon their nights blurred with planning
shed beers for thinking
scattered among bolts and sparks
her voice sparring with his grunts
her laughter cutting his doubt
sometimes she handed him scrap
sometimes she held it in place as he welded
her hands steady her trust unflinching
her presence no longer intrusion
but necessity

and when they fucked in the shed now
it was not only lust
it was part of the rhythm
her thighs gripping his waist
her moans spilling into the air
as if welding body to body
love to art fire to steel

afterwards lying tangled on the floor
he touched her face still smudged with dust
and whispered *you are not my muse*
you are my maker too
and she kissed him slow
smiling against his lips
then let us build not just steel harry
let us build a life that bends but never breaks

the shed was not enough anymore
council pieces came and went
gallery shows shone and faded
but harry and amanda dreamed of something bigger
not for money not for fame
but for the community that had raised them
both in different ways

amanda spread sketches across the workbench
coffee rings on the paper bolts scattered at the edges
she said *what if we build one not for them*
not for a cheque not for a council brief
but for us and for this place
something the community can stand inside
something they can touch and belong to

harry stared at the drawings
arches of steel curving like arms
figures interwoven strong and soft
he grunted low afraid of the scale
afraid of the hunger it awoke in him
this is bigger than us

she leaned close kissed his bearded jaw
then let us find the means to make it
you bend steel i bend words
between us we can do this

so she began the search
funding grants artist residencies
submissions thick with jargon
she sat cross-legged in the shed laptop open
swearing at forms that demanded timelines
swearing at budgets
that asked for what they could not yet name
harry watching her in awe
the same woman who straddled him fierce
was now straddling bureaucracy with sharper teeth

still the question of reach remained
their world was sparks and laughter
but money flowed through networks and names
and it was morgan who said over beer one night
i have a friend you should meet
alex martin sharp as a blade in arts networks
knows everyone worth knowing
she might open doors for you
so amanda called alex
a voice clear strong confident
and soon they sat in a café in adelaide
steel sketches spread across the table
alex leaning in her eyes bright
this is raw this is necessary she said
but you need to frame it in their language
talk about heritage talk about community health
talk about resilience and identity
and they will listen

harry shifted uncomfortably
muttering *i do not speak that way*
but amanda touched his thigh beneath the table
smiled at alex and said
then i will speak for him

and in that moment harry realised
their project was no longer only his
it was theirs
her voice his fire
steel and word welded into dream

alex martin did not waste time
her voice precise her stride sharp
she pulled them into meetings in adelaide
rooms where walls held canvases
and sculptures gleamed
where words like curation strategy and partnerships
spilled easier than sparks from steel

harry shifted in those rooms
boots too heavy shirt too ordinary
his hands rough still marked from the torch
he hated the way eyes slid over him
then back to amanda then to alex
as if he were only the brawn behind their polish

but amanda thrived
her voice quick her gaze steady
she spoke of resilience of heritage
of steel as survival of sculpture as memory
she drew lines between community health and creativity
between labour and beauty
and harry watched her astonished
as if she were welding with words
bending bureaucracy to her will

alex leaned on her networks
within the annual south australian living artists festival
the great sala exhibition spread across the state
hundreds of venues thousands of artists
and she told them *you can get in*
not just a small space but a feature
your warrior woman
and this new community project
side by side
eyes from all over south australia on you

alex explained that it was an open access festival
every one welcome
community based
finding a suitable venue
with venue finder online
but let us see who i know
who might have a special space
that will expose your work best

harry felt his stomach knot
the weight of so many eyes
the fear of being hollow beneath the praise
but amanda touched his wrist beneath the table
her voice low her smile fierce
we will not do this to be seen harry
we will do this to give them something to see

so the forms were filled the submissions made
alex smoothing language where needed
amanda sharpening vision where it dulled
harry sketching bending welding
his silence speaking louder than any speech

the day the acceptance came
a letter heavy with sala's seal
harry stood in the shed motionless
until amanda grabbed the paper laughed wild
and kissed him against the half-finished frame
her body pressed hard her voice husky in his ear
this is us harry
this is our fire reaching further than the shed
and you will not hide from it

and though fear still clung to his chest
he let himself believe
that maybe steel and love could both hold
under the weight of a festival panel's gaze
but what did it mean to be a finalist
always where there were wins
there were obligations

the shed was no longer theirs alone
deliveries arrived heavy with scrap and steel
volunteers curious neighbours friends
all wanting to see what else the festival would bring
what harry and amanda were making out of rust
and sweat

harry bristled at the noise
the shed had always been his sanctuary
his mask his only shield
but now eyes lingered too long
voices asked too many questions
and each weld felt exposed before it cooled

he worked longer hours sparks biting deeper
hands blistered back aching
but the silence of focus was gone
fear pressed hard against his ribs
fear of failing in front of so many
fear of being called not artist but fraud

amanda saw it
the way his shoulders locked the way his jaw clenched
so she fought her battles in rooms he would not enter
meetings with curators who wanted polish
emails from critics demanding statements
networking drinks where wine was poured like promises
she stood tall   her words quick
framing their vision in language the city understood
heritage resilience community identity
words that bent just as steel bent under torch

and when she came back late
her heels in her hand her hair falling loose
he kissed her as if she were air
lifting her onto the bench pulling her hips to him
their sex wild not just for lust
but to burn away the noise
to reclaim the fire as theirs alone

afterwards lying slick with sweat
she pressed her forehead to his chest
and whispered *you are the art harry*
not the critics not the curators not even the steel
you
and if they cannot see that
then they do not deserve you

but he shook his head his voice rough
and what if they see too much
what if i am only fire borrowed from you

her eyes flashed sharp her voice fierce
then let them see us
because i will not let you shrink
and i will not let them steal your fire

the shed rang with tension and laughter both
geralt dropping by with beer
morgan offering sharp wit
the aunties bringing sandwiches and gossip
their presence grounding
reminding harry that art was not only spotlight
but community holding him up

as the festival neared
the sculpture rose piece by piece
arms out wide a structure of steel that seemed alive
and harry realised with awe and dread both
that this time it was not only for them
it was for everyone

the whole state hummed with art that month
murals blooming across walls
paintings hung in cafes libraries streets
sculptures rising from parks and laneways
the festival sprawling like a flood
across south australia

and there in a winery in a hall white with light
harry's warrior woman stood fierce
the council piece gleaming beside her
and between them sketches and smaller forms
raw steel bent into arcs of resilience

the crowd was larger than harry had ever seen
critics with notebooks
families with children pulling free to touch the steel
students with cameras wide-eyed
and everywhere the murmur of voices
speaking his name speaking the word artist
as if it had always belonged to him

harry's stomach twisted
his boots heavy against polished floors
he longed for the hiss of his shed
for the quiet of dawn before fire broke silence
but amanda stood at his side
her hand steady at his back her gaze bright with pride

when the speeches began
curators praised resilience
heritage and community
alex's name mentioned in thanks
and amanda's words woven through the programme
harry felt the eyes press harder
his throat dry his palms rough against his thighs

then amanda stepped forward
her voice clear cutting through the hum
this is not just steel she said
this is labour made visible
this is fire transformed into care
this is the body of community
fighting surviving loving still

the hall hushed
her words ringing louder than applause
and harry realised with awe and dread both
that he was not only standing in front of art
he was standing in front of himself revealed

after the speeches
people pressed close
wanting his words his story his signature
he stumbled but amanda caught him
smiled wicked whispered low
you only need to say one thing harry
say thank you and let them see the fire in your eyes

so he did
each thank you rough but true
each handshake heavy but real
and when the night ended
when the crowd thinned and the hall emptied
he stood before the warrior woman again
her arms outstretched her steel strong
and whispered low so only amanda could hear
i am afraid of being seen
and she pressed her lips to his ear
then let them see us together

and in that moment
he knew the festival win was not exposure
it was belonging
not just his
but theirs

the festival had cracked something open
praise came in letters in calls in glowing words
opportunities spilled across their table
offers for more exhibitions
commissions from towns and cities
talk of residencies even travel abroad

harry stared at the papers with a frown
his boots heavy against the shed floor
his torch silent for days as he wrestled with the noise
he had always worked for fire not for applause
and now applause demanded more fire
than he could bear

amanda thrived in the storm
she danced through meetings
laughed with journalists
her words sharper each time she spoke of him
she could see the shape of a future
where his art lifted not only them
but the community that had birthed him
but she saw too the lines deepening on his face
the way his hands shook when he held the letters
the way his silence grew louder than sparks

one night after the phone rang again
with another offer too grand to ignore
he sat at the workbench head low
and muttered
i do not know what is mine anymore
is it the steel the sweat the shed
or do they all belong to them now
the world that claps and points and calls me artist

she climbed onto the bench straddled his lap
cupped his beard darkened face with both hands
and whispered
no harry
they can see the fire but they cannot own it
the shed is still ours
the bed is still ours
the morning coffees the aunties the laughter the scars
all ours
let them have the sculptures
but we keep the flame

his breath broke against her chest
fear loosening in her arms
and when they made love that night
it was slower than the festival pace
a reclaiming of skin and silence
each kiss a reminder of where the fire began

in the morning she brewed coffee
two mugs not one
and set the papers aside
her smile wicked her voice steady
we choose what we give
we choose what we keep
they cannot take us unless we hand ourselves over

and harry realised then
that balance was not between art and love
it was in the choosing
and together they would choose again
and again

alex arrived at the shed one evening
her voice brisk her eyes bright
you have done the council you have done sala
but now is the time to stretch wider
not only exhibit not only unveil
but teach and tour

she spread papers across the bench
proposals for a state-wide exhibition
steel pieces travelling town to town
schools invited into the making
workshops where children would hold the torch
where farmers would see themselves in the steel
where women would see their fight
in the warrior's stance

harry's chest tightened as he scanned the pages
months on the road months away from the shed
crowds and faces and voices always pressing
the thought of it burned his stomach raw
this is not me he muttered
i am not built for stages and schedules
i am built for sparks and silence

but amanda's eyes lit with fire
her voice low and fierce
this is not only about you harry
this is about teaching them
that steel is survival that art is labour
that care and fight can be welded together
you have fire in your hands
and now you have the chance to pass the torch

still he shook his head
fear like rust eating slow
what if i lose the fire on the road
what if i lose us
she cupped his face his beard soft on her palms
and whispered *then we take us with us*
we fuck in motel rooms
we laugh in council halls
we wake before dawn in borrowed sheds
and we carry our fire everywhere

the aunties heard about it and clapped their hands
shirley saying *about bloody time he gave something back*
sheila nodding through tears
pat smirking *you are both already a travelling circus*
geralt roared with laughter
morgan raised her glass
alex only smiled her glorious smile
the work will speak for itself she said
but you must carry it further than these four walls

that night harry and amanda lay tangled in sweat
the shed humming quiet
he pressed his lips to her temple
his voice rough as gravel
if we do this i am betting it all again
not just the art not just the fire
but you
and she kissed him deep
her voice steady against his mouth
then bet it all harry
because i am betting too

the road stretched long across south australia
from small towns tucked between vines
to schools standing against dry paddocks
to halls that smelled of dust and history

alex's networks had laid the path
but it was harry and amanda who carried the fire

the first workshop nearly broke him
rows of teenagers fidgeting wide-eyed
helmets too large gloves stiff on their hands
harry stood before them torch in grip
his throat tight palms damp
he had never been a man for speeches
his fire was silence his language sparks
and now all eyes waited on him

amanda stepped in as she always did
her voice weaving sharp and warm
this is steel she told them
this is what labour looks like when it bends into art
harry here has spent his life welding
not for galleries but for survival
today you get to hold the fire yourselves

the students leaned forward
and when harry finally lit the torch
the hiss filled the room
and the first sparks flew
their faces lit with awe
the fear in his chest softened into something new
something like pride

he guided their hands
steadying the torch
showing how to listen for the hiss
how to see the glow change colour
each one nervous each one brave
and when a small girl looked up through the mask
her voice muffled but clear
i made it stick
he felt his chest crack open
satisfaction fierce and full
different from the rush of exhibitions
different from sex and sweat
a deeper fire
knowing he had given something they could carry

on the road amanda was his anchor
her laughter filling motel rooms
her heels abandoned at hall doors
her voice fierce in town meetings
she translated his silence into vision
and when they fucked in beds too small
their moans muffled by thin walls
they reclaimed what the road tried to take
their intimacy welded anew each night

at one school the aunties even came along
shirley bossing the kids around
sheila fussing over helmets
pat smirking when sparks flew wide
the shed had become mobile
their family stretched across country roads

and harry realised teaching was not the theft of his fire
it was its multiplication
each child who held the torch
each farmer who nodded at the steel rising
each woman who saw herself in the warrior's stance
then had a go with the flame
they all carried a spark home

and when he and amanda sat one evening
by the side of a dusty road
coffee in enamel mugs
her head on his shoulder
he whispered low
maybe this is the most satisfying thing i have ever done
and she kissed his neck
her voice soft and certain
then we keep going harry
because fire only grows when it is shared

the touring wore them down
motel beds too small too soft
coffee from thermoses lukewarm
early mornings hauling scrap into borrowed sheds
late nights driving dark roads with eyes half-closed
harry's back ached
his hands blistered raw from guiding new fingers
his voice hoarse from words he was not used to speaking
amanda's body tired
her heels abandoned more often than worn
her days filled with endless talking
with smoothing timetables chasing funding
managing faces

and yet
each town met them with open arms
farmers arriving in dusty utes
mothers bringing children who had never seen sparks fly
teenagers restless and shy until they held the torch
elders pressing his calloused hands whispering
we see ourselves in this steel

harry felt his exhaustion crack and lift each time
their awe sharper than any critic's words
their gratitude a weight he could carry
and when he crawled into bed at night
his body breaking his eyes heavy
amanda curled against him warm

her whisper steady
we are not only showing art harry
we are planting fire
and it will outlive us

sometimes their sex was hurried desperate
a reclaiming of intimacy before sleep took them
sometimes it was slow deliberate
a reminder that even on the road
their bodies belonged not to the world but to each other
and always it was the anchor
the way they remembered why they had begun

the aunties phoned often
their voices sharp and warm
shirley barking *do not forget to eat harry*
sheila fussing over his back   his sleep
pat teasing amanda
bet you never thought you'd be touring with a welder
their laughter through the line grounding him again

and as the months stretched long
as the maps filled with pins
harry realised teaching and touring was not theft of fire
it was its spreading
and though it wore him thin
though it pulled at their bones
it was also satisfying
in a way the shed alone had never been

for the first time in his life
harry felt part of something larger than himself
and he knew it was because amanda had set the match
and refused to let him hide from the flame

the tour had carried them through halls
and schools and paddocks
but now it led them into boardrooms
into offices where suits sat at long tables
where words like accountability outcomes deliverables
were wielded sharper than knives

harry sat stiff in those rooms
his boots leaving marks on polished floors
his hands itching for a torch
not a pen not a contract
but it was amanda who leaned forward
eyes alight voice steady
facing down the questions
the doubts
the thin smiles

because some wanted to use them
wanted the warrior woman's strength
without the fight that birthed her
wanted resilience without naming struggle
wanted beauty without scars

one official said sneeringly
art is an expensive addition   a nice frill
and harry's jaw clenched so hard it ached
but amanda's laugh rang sharp
art is not the frill on the frock of life she said
art is the frock the skin the blood
art is what makes you proud
art is what holds communities together
without art we are just surviving
with art we are alive

the room stilled
eyes shifting uneasily
and harry felt something stir deep
a roar he had never used in words
but in sparks and sweat he had always known
so he leaned forward his voice rough
when you put steel in a child's hands
and they see it bend under fire
they stand taller
that is not a frill
that is life

the silence after was heavy
but alex caught his eye and nodded
and amanda's hand slid across the table
squeezing his under the wood unseen

afterwards in the car park
he groaned his shoulders sagging
but amanda laughed kissed his cheek
and whispered
see
you do not always need the shed
to make sparks
sometimes your words burn too

that night in the motel bed
they fucked with laughter still in their mouths
her moans spilling into his chest
his hands gripping her thighs
their rhythm less frantic more triumphant
a release not only of lust
but of pressure and pride
the knowledge that they had not bowed
that they had carried their truth into the coldest room
and lit it on fire

the tour had lit towns and schools
children still writing letters weeks later
farmers still sending photos of small welds in their sheds
elders still thanking them for giving voice to resilience
and word travelled further than they expected

first came calls from melbourne
then sydney then brisbane
arts councils interstate curious about the warrior woman
curious about the workshops
that turned sparks into pride
offers for teaching tours for exhibitions for residencies
all with travel all with months away from home

amanda read each email with fire in her eyes
her fingers tapping excited across the keyboard
her mind already sketching maps of possibility
this could be bigger harry she said
this could carry our message across the country
art is not the frill on the frock of life
it is the cloth it is the thread it is everything
imagine if we told that truth from coast to coast

but harry's chest grew heavy
his boots felt heavier still
he thought of the shed silent waiting
he thought of the aunties bringing biscuits and gossip
he thought of mornings in their bed
coffee steaming soft laughter between kisses
and he wondered how far they could go
before they lost the centre that made them fire

one night he muttered
what if we travel so far we forget where we started
what if the world swallows us whole
what if i am not meant for planes and schedules
what if i am only meant for steel in my shed

amanda climbed across him in the motel bed
her hair wild her body hot against his
she kissed him slow then hard
and whispered
then we carry the shed with us
we carry the coffee the laughter the aunties
we weld ourselves wherever we land
because fire does not belong to one place alone
fire belongs to whoever holds it

her words settled deep
and when they made love that night
it was not desperate not rushed
but slow deliberate
as if to remind him
that home was not walls of tin or smell of sparks
home was her hips her laugh her hand in his

still harry's question lingered
how far could they carry the fire
before the world tried to claim it as its own

invitations piled like sparks too quick to catch
perth darwin hobart
offers with airfares and stipends
words like national platform
and cultural impact

amanda's eyes glowed when she read them
her hands quick her mind alive with possibility
harry listened heavy
the shed whispering behind him
the weight of home pulling at his boots

the aunties noticed before he spoke
shirley called first
harry you sound tired on the line
sheila worried   fussing
pat only smirked wryly
you two better come round
before you forget who you are

so they gathered in the shed one friday night
biscuits on plates
mugs of tea strong enough to strip paint
geralt sprawled on a crate morgan perched sharp-eyed
stainless steel gleaming in the corner

harry tried to explain
his words rough tumbling
how the world wanted more
how he feared giving too much
how he feared leaving what held him steady

the aunties listened without interruption
then shirley barked out
art is not a holiday harry
you do not wander off and leave us behind
if you go you take us with you
because the fire started here
sheila's voice was gentler
the world needs to see what you have built
but never forget the shed is not tin and sparks
the shed is us
and we will always be here when you return
pat leaned forward her smile sharp
fire grows when you feed it
but a fire that leaves its hearth dies quick
find your balance harry
take her hand take your work
but remember where you struck the first match

amanda squeezed his thigh beneath the table
her voice low and sure
they are right harry
we can carry the fire anywhere
but we must always bring it back home

geralt raised his beer bottle in salute
morgan grinned and said
do not worry harry
you will not be swallowed by the world
you are too bloody stubborn for that

the shed rang with laughter and truth
and harry felt the knot in his chest loosen
for the first time he believed
that travelling did not mean losing
that the world could see his fire
and still it would belong to them all

that night in their bed
amanda straddled him slow
her voice husky against his ear
home is not a place harry
home is this fire we make together
and as he came undone beneath her
he whispered *yes*
believing it

the road out of adelaide curved east
past paddocks pale with winter
past vines stripped bare
past towns that knew their names already
from social media and whispers

harry gripped the wheel of the old ute
welding unit strapped tight on the trailer behind
his hands steady but his chest uneasy
he had never crossed state lines for fire
never left the aunties the shed the coast behind
he muttered more than once
what if the sparks do not travel
what if the flame dies on strange ground

amanda rested her hand on his thigh
her voice calm but fierce
fire does not belong to dirt or shed
fire belongs to whoever lights it
and we will light it again and again

their first stop was a small town outside melbourne
a borrowed hall that smelled of sweaty shoes and dust
rows of children waiting helmets too big for their heads
farmers curious leaning in the doorway
teachers whispering nervously about safety forms

harry's throat tightened as always
but the moment the torch hissed to life
the fear thinned into smoke
sparks lit wide eyes
a girl whispered *it looks like stars*
a boy shouted *i made it stick*
and pride filled him fierce and sharp
satisfaction flooding faster than exhaustion

that night in a motel that smelled of stale carpet
amanda sprawled naked across the bed
her laugh loud her eyes wild
see harry she teased
the sparks travel fine
and he bent over her
his mouth tracing fire down her stomach
his tongue drawing moans from her lips
until the walls shook with their rhythm
a reminder that no matter how far the road stretched
their home was here in sweat and heat and laughter

letters followed them even there
parents writing thanks
students drawing pictures of flames
the aunties phoning to gossip and scold
shirley barking *keep your head harry*
sheila telling amanda to feed him proper
pat snickering
morgan told you the world would not swallow you whole
their voices weaving the thread of home across the miles

and harry realised
lying spent with amanda curled against him
that home was not lost when you left it
home was carried in steel and in skin
home was in the sparks you shared with others
home was in the woman
who would not let you hide from the fire

the interstate journey swelled larger than they expected
not just halls and schools but theatres galleries plazas
crowds thick enough to blur into noise
critics with pens sharp as knives
reporters eager for the story of the welder turned artist
the warrior woman multiplied into headlines
her steel frame a symbol people wanted to claim

amanda thrived in the storm
her voice polished her smile sure
she met curators with wit
she charmed journalists with fire
she bent politics to their vision
with words as steady as steel

harry stood in the glow but did not glow himself
each clap each camera flash pressed heavy
his hands longed for the hiss of the torch
the quiet rhythm of sparks on steel
not questions about meaning
not speeches about vision
he muttered more than once to amanda
success feels like weight not wings

one night after a crowd so thick he could barely breathe
they collapsed into a hotel bed high above the city
lights glittering below like fallen stars
amanda curled against his chest
her voice husky with exhaustion
you were brilliant today she said
but he shook his head rough
i was not
i was noise in a room already full of noise

she lifted her head met his eyes
no harry
you were fire in a room that thought itself cold
you think success is a burden
but burden is only proof you are carrying
something that matters

still doubt gnawed
in the morning as he stared at the skyline
he whispered low
what if i lose myself in all this
what if i forget the shed the aunties the coffee
what if i forget us

amanda slid her arms around him from behind
pressed her lips to his shoulder
and murmured
then i will remind you
every night every morning
in motel beds and borrowed sheds
in laughter and in sweat
because success will not swallow you
not while i am here to burn beside you

that night their sex was slower
not frantic not desperate
but a reclaiming of silence
her moans soft her nails light on his skin
his thrusts steady his forehead pressed to hers
a rhythm not for the world not for applause
but for them alone

and in the quiet after
as the city roared below
harry realised success might be heavy
but with her it did not break him
with her it became something else
a weight worth carrying

the tour ended not with applause but with silence
the ute rattled back across the border
into south australia
the welding unit lighter in the trailer
their bodies weary their eyes full of places and faces
letters stuffed in boxes drawings from children
parents' notes folded soft with fingerprints
all proof of fire carried and left behind

when the shed came into view
harry stopped the ute and simply stared
the metal walls leaned familiar
the warrior woman still standing sentinel
but here the ground felt truer
sparks already waiting in the dust
his throat tightened
home he whispered
and amanda touched his arm
ours she said

the aunties came that night
shirley with a plate of biscuits
sheila with soup still steaming
pat with a wry grin and a flask tucked in her bag
they fussed they teased they laughed until tears spilled

harry you look older shirley said
pat smirked *you look more alive*
and amanda only laughed with them
her voice weaving into their chorus
as if she had always belonged

geralt and morgan followed
boots heavy jokes loud
beer bottles clinking against the workbench
stories spilling of what the papers had written
but what mattered most
was the way they all sat in the shed
as if it had never been empty of their voices

harry felt it then
success had stretched them thin
but home stitched them whole again
and he realised it was never about choosing
never about art or love or community alone
it was about the weaving
steel and sweat and laughter and touch
fire carried together

that night after the crowd had gone
the shed quiet again
he and amanda stood in the glow of the torch
the flame hissing steady

and he whispered
i am not afraid anymore
not of success not of failure not of being seen
because whatever happens
we build it together

she kissed him slow
her voice husky with truth
then let us keep building harry
not just steel not just fire
but mornings and nights and every spark between
because the shed is not walls
the shed is us

and when they lay down on the cool floor
her thighs wrapping around him
their bodies meeting with the same hunger
as the first time
they knew the future was not certain
but it was theirs
a fire that would not go out

part two
forging of courage and truth

she began as silence unseen and unnamed
and became voice that claimed her own skin
her story woven in courage and flight
in freedom and in fire of becoming whole

chapter one

colin sips his latte at saltbush city limits café
the milk slides against his tongue sweet bitter desirable
outside through the wide window
his own metal work rises into the blue
a sturt desert pea rusted iron stretching skyward
circles welded recycled discs singing sun
the flower boss gleams stainless mesh against the brown
dominating the gibber stones the saltbush roots
his pride his name his hunger
trading on someone else's reputation

for months he has begged the owner
let me show my work
let me sell let me be seen
today it stands tall his favourite his proof
a mark upon the land a sign of himself
metal made promise of fortune to come
in this dry town where dreams rust quick
where a man must push his art against the dust

he thinks of the pieces he makes to order
names embossed on curling leaves of iron
flowers hammered from industrial shades
shining spheres stacked two metres high
roses that woo lovers
roses that guarantee a gobby
roses that open thighs
each petal each weld a bid for glory
each sale a ticket to pleasure

he buys more coffee more cake
carrot spice cream cheese on his tongue
sweetness sliding sharp hunger stirred
the taste makes him horny
he grins to himself

looking good she says
a female voice soft but dangerous
he turns his chair her blue eyes blaze
you came he whispers
careful careful this small town
her ringed hands her bracelets clinking
her blonde hair falling to her waist
her mouth curved in secrecy
she holds her own coffee
asks if she may sit

he pulls out a chair thrill shivers his bulk
to sit with her in daylight a daring act
for always they meet hidden
among the welders and grinders
her body pressed against cold steel benches
sweat and sparks on his skin
her moans swallowed by metal echoes
never at her home in quilpie
where her husband the opal miner waits
his fists his rage his name

colin twenty six restless
ten years of experimental lust
not ready for any home or any child
not ready for any chains
he fears her husband
he fears himself

yet he drinks her in anyway
he likes this life the edge of it
the taste of risk the taste of her
his father would sneer
tell him *get a real job a family*
but colin will not bend to that fate
no house no mortgage no children
only art only lust only the fire of metal
and money
it's all about the money

it looks really great she says
tilting her head at his creation
her bracelets catching the light
her delicate strong hands curling the cup
her eyes glittering
as though she too were welded flame

under john waugh bridge on the bulloo river
a new year's eve gathering
gas barbecues spitting fat
too much meat too much drink
friends of friends toasting the turning of time
the night thick with beer breath and laughter

colin leaning against a pillar
thinking of leaving drifting away
until she found him her body swaying
twenty years older a little tipsy
but her eyes blue sparks her mouth curved guiltily
she asked if he wanted fun
always he said the word a spark
igniting something raw

they walked the path by the river
to the wooden bird hide shadows deep
planks creaking night air hot
she pulled him through the doorway
pressed him back on the narrow seat
unzipped his jeans with steady hands

her tongue on him sudden fire
the best gobby of his life
he gasped grabbed wood for balance
then she climbed him rode him hard
her fingers pinching his nipples for hold
his breath ragged his body burning
the river sliding past outside
the bridge looming iron dark above

he thought briefly of john waugh
and the men who built this span
their sweat their grit their calloused hands
surely they never dreamed of this
lust breaking open in their shadow

condoms flickered across his mind
but he let the thought fall away
no talk no barrier only skin on skin
only need devouring need

now he is hooked
sex with her a drug sharp and urgent
he needs the fix
he needs her again and again

congrats she says tilting her head again
towards the rusted magnificence outside
the sturt desert pea gleaming against sky and stone

thanks he murmurs hope rising and falling
now i just need a tourist or anyone at all
to grab a card from the counter
to call me to order some metal art
i could use the money only one order last month
his words heavy with need and the taste of scarcity

they will she laughs bracelets chiming
do not worry about that
her mouth leans close pouty lips trembling promise
now let us go back to your workshop she whispers
and celebrate

is that an order he teases grin curling his face
is that an order ma'am she playfully corrects
yes yes it is

being with her is a rush
exhilaration pounding his chest
a sweetness flooding his veins
every time her fingers brush his skin
his whole body shivers awake
colin has never known a woman like her
never known a fire so consuming
she makes him reckless
she makes him hungry
crazy for her in ways that tear at his sleep
and shake him from the inside out

not like this not ever before
other women wanted the house
the children the ordinary life
but she wants the moment
she wants the secret
she wants him rough and unclaimed
and he cannot resist her
his blood burns his mind bends
his art even feels different
as if her lust welds itself into his steel

yet always at the edges
fear prowls sharp and certain
because she belongs to nobby
and nobby is a man made of danger
broad arms muscled from the mines
eyes black with suspicion
a man who drinks hard fights harder
a man whose silence is a threat
a man whose rage explodes without warning
opal miner hands that can crush stone
opal miner hands that can crush him

colin has seen what happens in quilpie
to men who cross the line
faces split in pub carparks
bones broken and buried
rumours of men who disappeared
out past the gibber flats
the desert swallowing their names

he knows without doubt
if nobby finds out about her
about their bodies colliding in the dark
about the secrets spilled between gasps
he will kill them
simple as breathing
a punch a blade a bullet in the night
death certain as rust in iron

so colin lives on the edge of two flames
exhilaration and terror
lust and fear
desire devouring him alive
dread curling inside his stomach
yet he cannot stop
cannot turn away
the risk is the hook
the danger the drug
and she is the fire
that keeps him coming back

yet he keeps on with her
keeps dragging her body against his
even as his mind whispers *stop*
bad idea stop now before it breaks you
still he does not listen
because his cock his tongue his hands
refuse to obey
because every nerve in him screams for her
every day every hour

in the workshop
the smell of hot steel thick
sparks from the grinder
still hot on the bench
rust dust clings to his boots
she presses him back
against a cold sheet of iron
mouth devouring him
hands quick urgent
he moans into her hair
the taste of sweat
the clang of tools
falling around them

he tells himself again this will end badly
this will burn him alive
nobby's name echoes like hammer blows
danger rising in his gut
but then her lips slide lower
her rings glint against his skin
and he is gone again
lost in the wet heat of her mouth
the hard thrust of her hips
the scrape of her nails across his chest

he knows it is trouble
knows it will come for him one day
but he cannot stop
he must taste her again and again
no matter the cost
no matter the shadow
waiting
just beyond the door

chapter six

their lips meet
the moment they cross the threshold
steel air thick with heat and dust
colin closes his eyes drinks her in
the sliding door left wide open behind him
but nothing matters now
only her mouth only the taste of her breath
only the fire spilling into him

his shaking fingers clumsy on her bra
panting words pressed between kisses
i thought you could not get out today
isn't nobby home

he is she murmurs lips grazing his skin
asleep from the night shift
reckons the summer air is cooler then
reckons his sweat belongs to the darkness

her laugh low against his throat
her body pressing closer
her hands tugging his shirt free
danger dripping through every kiss
fear and lust braided into one
as the open door gapes behind them
and still he does not stop
still he cannot stop

two weeks since he last touched her
two weeks of dreaming sweating longing

her taste still burning on his tongue
her scent still caught in his clothes
nights restless with memory
days heavy with hunger

their words slip back and forth on signal
the secret app he trusts to hide them

untraceable he believes
no little dots pulsing like heartbeat
but each message a jolt a fix a promise

he told her of the sturt desert pea
rising at saltbush city limits café
rusted petals stainless mesh
his pride hammered into steel
knowing she could not risk seeing it
not with eyes watching in this small town

he sent her photos anyway
metal sections
sprawled across his workshop floor

sheets and scraps welded into meaning
another shot of the whole creation

strapped and waiting on the back of his ute
like proof of his hands like proof of his name
and also a lure
a reminder
a whisper of him

she sends back a photo
her face tilted her lips turned down
a sad little mask of longing
words beneath it saying she cannot get out
not today not tomorrow
her husband home
restless in the heat

she dares only when he is gone
when the opal claim swallows him whole
or when travel takes him
down the red roads
then she slips free like smoke
into colin's arms into colin's fire
but with nobby home her body is locked away
her hunger shuttered behind walls of fear

colin stares at the photo
stares at the curve of her mouth
the sadness in her eyes
and feels both ache and fury rise in him
two weeks too long
two weeks too empty
and still she is only a picture
only pixels hiding in his phone

even when she dares to slip away
they move like shadows careful cautious
because nobby's eyes are everywhere
his mates thick across quilpie
watchful loyal quick to talk

the opal miners scattered through the town
grubby overalls streaked with brown dust
sweaty singlets clinging to broad chests
faces burnt by sun and suspicion

they stand in line at the bottle shop
they nod at the post office counter
they push trolleys through foodworks' aisles
their utes rattle down unmade roads
past mullock heaps and gidgee scrub
men of stone and sweat
men who see everything

every corner every glance
a risk a whisper a possibility
that one word will slide back to nobby
and end them both

paranoia coils around him tight
every glance in town feels sharp
every nod from a miner a question
every laugh behind his back a threat

he imagines nobby's shadow in the bottle shop
nobby's boots heavy on the post office floor
nobby's ute growling behind him on the track
brown dust storm rising in the rearview mirror

rage strapped behind the wheel
when her text signal pings
he checks twice
then deletes the words
then deletes again

as if erasing could undo desire
as if fear could kill the need
but the hunger only grows
his cock hard even as his gut knots
his hands trembling when he welds
because he sees her face in the flame
and hears nobby's name in the grinder's whine

every time she leans close he thinks
who saw who noticed who will tell
every kiss carries the taste of danger
every fuck carries the weight of death
and still he goes back still he takes her
because terror sharpens the lust
and paranoia becomes its own drug

paranoia keeps him company
a whisper stitched beneath the skin
he counts the steps
between the shed and the gate
hears engines where there are none
the rattle of chains in the wind
a screen glow becomes a warning
a message a trap
he scrubs her name from his phone
but her scent stays on his hands
oil and sweat and sin

he lies awake listening for tyres on gravel
for the cough of that ute in the dark
for the knock that never comes but always will
he dreams of nobby's face in the flame
jaw clenched eyes cold as steel
and wakes choking on smoke that isn't there
his heart hammering like a weld gone wrong

the mask of fear fused to his skin
he tells himself he can stop
tells himself next time will be the last
but the wanting is a wound
he picks until it bleeds
and every spark in the shed
writes her name across the night

he knows the sickness now
how it threads through him
fear and wanting the same pulse
the same fevered breath
he tells himself it's love
but it's panic dressed in skin
her touch a match
struck in a gas filled room
his need feeding the fire
his dread fanning it higher

he can't stop
because the fear is what keeps him alive
because without the chase
without the shadow behind him
the lust would die
and so he stays burning
paranoia his lover
desire his cage

desperate for her he trembles in need
and she soothes him with a whisper
i told him i am seeing a friend today
it is not even a lie
and i do not care anymore if he finds out
i am sick of being only nobby's wife
i want a life of my own

her words ignite him
a promise reckless and raw
a freedom that tastes of fire

he strips off his t-shirt
her hands seize his chest
fingers tight on his nipples
a gasp breaks from his throat

he tears at her blouse
buttons flying ricocheting
against the iron bolted machines
clattering like sparks in the dim
she closes her eyes arches her back
moans spilling into the steel air
as his hands roam greedy urgent
as the workshop swallows their sounds

his hands seize her breasts
flesh warm against his palms
her bra tossed down
landing in the grit of the concrete floor
he fists her hair pulls her head back
his mouth tracing fire along her neck
the smell of her skin drowning him
his heart a hammer in his chest
each beat a warning each beat a surrender

you cannot he whispers broken between breaths
you cannot let him know
he will kill us both without pause
his words tremble even as his hands do not

she gasps as he slides beneath her skirt
finds the edge of her bikini pants
fingers curling like claws of want
then rips them free
fabric tearing sharp in the air
her moan colliding with the clang of machines
desire louder than dread
and still the shadow of nobby lurks
like a blade waiting in the dust

he shoves her back against the cold metal bench
steel biting into her skin as he lifts her high
leans over her naked torso
mouth closing on her breast
eyes shut lost in the fragrance of her sweat
the salt of her skin the sweetness of sin

his belt clatters loose
zip sliding down denim
no tighty whities for colin never
only flesh hard urgent bare

he groans deep as he eases inside her
her body opening her legs rising
wrapping around his neck
part choke part embrace
each pulse each thrust
her arching body driving him wilder
air hot lungs burning
lust louder than reason

oh colin oh colin
her voice breaking into moans
echoing off the bolted machines
danger forgotten desire ruling all

the burn rises fierce inside him
every nerve lit every vein alive
he is close so close
her moans rise higher her body thrashing
his thrusts urgent wild without rhythm
the heat building the edge breaking

then suddenly her scream
sharp as metal tearing
she shoves him hard
his body stumbling back
balance gone legs buckling
he crashes to the concrete
the thud echoing through the workshop
his jeans gaping his cock exposed
the air chill against the sweat of his skin

desire ripped away in a heartbeat
replaced with confusion raw
fear stabbing through the haze
her cry still ringing in his ears
the taste of climax
turned bitter in his mouth

chapter fifteen

what the fuck he gasps
scrambling raw on the filthy floor
jeans gaping breath ragged
her scream still tearing the air

then he sees it
sees why her voice broke into terror
a set of eyes drilling down into him
not just any eyes
but cold menacing eyes
the kind that strip you bare
the kind that promise consequence

senior sergeant geralt chadowski
standing in the open doorway
boots planted heavy arms folded tight
authority thick as iron in his frame
the law itself
staring straight into colin's shame

blood drains from colin's face
lust shrivels in his gut
fear swallows everything whole
caught exposed undone
nothing to hide behind now

the workshop air feels freezing
metal scent sharp and unforgiving
her blouse half torn her chest rising fast
colin sprawling on the concrete
zip open
shame raw between them

geralt's eyes narrow a glint of steel
his voice low deliberate cutting
so this is what you call art colin
fucking another man's wife
between the welders and the grinders
selling knock offs and spreading your filth
happy if her lips are soft and she gets you off

every word lands like a hammer blow
colin tries to speak but his throat locks
his tongue thick useless
the sergeant steps closer
boots striking concrete like gunshots
shadow falling long across the floor

you thought no one was watching
you thought you could steal designs
and fuck who you please
but the bush talks boy
and the bush talks loud

her gasp shatters against the silence
her hands clutching at loose fabric
eyes wide with terror
but geralt does not look at her
his stare pins colin alone
like an insect skewered to steel

the corrugated iron walls hum with heat again
flies thick as dust motes
the woman sits silent on an upturned crate
colin's welding mask
hung like a ghost on the nail behind her
a half-finished sculpture crouches in shadow
steel bones bent toward something almost human

and geralt chadowski stands in the doorway
his shadow looming
no badge power here
no jurisdiction in quilpie
but loyalty doesn't need paperwork

stern brown eyes that see through
bluster and bullshit
broad shouldered
thick as the trunks of ironbark
his beard a wild territory of its own
dark shot through with copper and dust

hair locked tight in thick ropes
shaved close above the ears
patterns carved like runes of protection
a viking warrior misplaced in the arid zone
his boots sinking deep into red sand
flies orbiting his sweat-slick neck
a presence that bent the heat around him
half myth half man
and entirely sure of where he stood

the locals stared
when he strode down the single street
some said he was here for the opal
others whispered he hunted ghosts
but only he knew the truth
that loyalty to a mate
runs deeper than distance
that even out here
where the wind forgets names
a man like geralt chadowski
carries his own weather

he has come chasing whispers
of an artist flogging fakes
passing harry flugelman's sweat and fire
as his own invention
marketplace listings slick with lies
and geralt's not having it
not while harry's back is still sore
from grinding truth into shape

geralt's boots scuff the dirt floor
colin looks up
eyes wary but steady
you're a long way from home sergeant

yeah geralt says
and you're a long way from clever
selling fakes at half the prices
and not even half as good
the silence after is thick enough to hold a storm

outside the horizon burns pale
inside the shed
the truth is welding itself together
slow sparks of fear
and loyalty
and something like redemption
as geralt realises
the woman isn't the thief
his gaze shifts from colin to the woman
then to the figure half-born beside her
geralt sees her twice
once in flesh and once in steel

so this is what you've been doing colin
not just stealing designs
but shaping them around her
turning theft into confession

colin doesn't answer
his jaw tight
his hands raw from the grinder
the woman keeps her eyes low
the sculpture between them a mirror
of what none of them can admit

geralt steps closer
heat and silence closing in
this isn't about art anymore
it's about truth
and who's got the right to make it

the light flickers
catches on a curve of metal
something tender in the angle
not accident not luck
but longing shaped by hand

geralt sees it now
in the way colin breathes
half ashamed of what he's done
as if creation were confession
as if beauty were betrayal

geralt feels the weight shift
the fight gone out of the air
this man wasn't just building armour
he was building a mirror
and didn't know it yet

he looks once more at the shoulders
too honest to be fake
and mutters
harry would've seen it too
would've known
that even in men like this
art burns beneath the fear

chapter seventeen

geralt does not blink
his voice drops lower darker
the kind of tone that carries to graves
he's got no jurisdiction in quilpie
but he doesn't need it
he's here on the old law
the one called loyalty

you think i have not been watching
he says slow deliberate
i have seen your work boy
seen it passed off as harry's
and you sell them as flugelman originals
on facebook of all places
cheap trick cheap fraud

geralt takes a step closer
his shadow swallows colin whole
you think the miners do not talk
you think a wife can slip away unseen
every beer every smoke
every dusty road carries news
nobby hears it all
and when he does
there will not be enough left of you
to sweep into a bag

the woman whimpers
pulls fabric tight across her chest
but geralt does not flinch does not even glance
his eyes drill only into colin
the weight of theft adultery betrayal
stacking high like ore ready to crush

you wanted a carefree life colin
you wanted lust without consequence
but lust is never free
art is never free
every weld has its weakness
and i am here to snap yours clean

colin's mouth opens but no sound comes
his chest heaves shallow desperate
sweat dripping into the grime on the floor
eyes darting anywhere
but the sergeant's stare

i did not mean to he stammers at last
the words thin weak sliding from his lips
it is not like that not really
i only wanted a chance a bit of money
a bit of fun
i did not think it would matter
i did not think anyone would notice

his hands tremble clawing at his open jeans
trying to cover himself
trying to gather the scraps of his dignity
but the more he moves the more he shakes
his voice cracks raw with pleading

i was going to stop i swear
no more copies no more lies
no more her
his eyes flick to the woman
who shrinks away arms folded tight
her face pale her lips pressed closed

please geralt please
his tone shrivels into begging
like a boy cornered
like a thief caught with crumbs on his chin
you cannot tell nobby
he will kill me
he will kill us both

the workshop holds the silence
machines bolted down like witnesses
the smell of iron sharp in the air
colin kneeling broken
his weakness splayed bare
before the law of loyalty
before desire before ruin

geralt looks down at him
eyes flat as iron dark as coal
no pity no mercy
only the weight of judgment

pathetic he mutters
voice low but sharp enough to cut
you talk of art
but all i see is a thief on his knees
a coward with his cock hanging out
a boy who plays at being a man
and fails at both

colin whimpers tries to answer
but geralt raises a hand
silence cracks like a whip
you think i care for your excuses
you think anyone will remember your words
they will remember only what you did
stealing from a mate
fucking a wife
shitting on trust and loyalty
for a scrap of money
for a wet hole in the dark

geralt leans closer
boots grinding into the concrete
his face inches from colin's
i have seen hard men in this town
men who mine until their lungs bleed
men who bury mates in dust storms
men who fight and drink
and still keep their honour
you are not one of them
you never will be

the words hang heavy
colin's shoulders sag beneath them
his mouth working empty
his body shrunken small
on the workshop floor
the copper's contempt colder than death
burning deeper than any fist

geralt straightens slowly
his shadow lifting but his scorn heavier still
look at you he says
sprawled like a dog that has been kicked
and still you beg for scraps

you think this town owes you something
you think art will hide your weakness
but metal does not lie boy
steel tells the truth
and your hands are not honest
every weld you stole
screams louder than your excuses

he circles colin
like a hawk above a crippled rabbit
do you even know what loyalty means
do you know what it costs to build trust
in a place like this
men give their blood for it
bury their dead for it
and you throw it away for a cheap fuck
and a pocket full of lies

his words echo off the bolted machines
sharp unforgiving
colin cringes beneath them
his eyes wet his lips trembling
but no answer comes
only the silence of shame
only the smell of sweat and fear

geralt's voice lowers to a growl
nobby will have your balls on a hook
when he finds out
and do not think i will stop him
a man like him lives by his own law
and a man like you
does not deserve the protection of mine

chapter twenty one

her voice slices through the heavy air
enough she cries *enough*
her chest heaving her eyes blazing
no longer the secret lover trembling in corners
but a woman cracked open raw

do not talk like i am not here
do not spit your contempt at him alone
i chose this i chose him
i am sick of being just nobby's wife
a shadow in his house
a name that belongs to someone else

she steps forward hair wild
fingers clutching torn fabric but her voice steady
i will not live only to cook his meals
to wash his clothes
to watch him drink himself hollow every night
while i rot invisible beside him
i want a life that is mine
do you hear me
mine

geralt's eyes narrow but she does not stop
if nobby kills us both then so be it
better dead than caged
better shamed than silent
i will not hide anymore

the words slam against the workshop walls
louder than the clang of steel
shaking the silence to its bones
colin stares up at her
astonished terrified aroused
his cowardice stripped bare against her fury
while geralt's jaw tightens
the air between them thick with something new

colin blinks up at her
as if the woman before him is not the same
who whispered in dark corners
who moaned against cold steel benches
her words hit him like sparks to dry grass
fury wild reckless alive

his mouth opens closes
nothing fits the moment
he stammers *i   i did not know*
his voice cracks
you never said it like that
you never told me you hated him so much
his hands tremble as if trying to hold her fire
but his fingers only clutch air

he glances at geralt then back at her
confusion swimming in his face
fear and awe tangled together
this is not the weak accomplice he thought
not just nobby's wife sneaking into his shed
but a storm that could burn down the town

his heart lurches
part terror part hunger
he whispers *what are you doing*
his words small lost
because he cannot match her rage
cannot carry her defiance
he is a boy watching a woman blaze

chapter twenty three

she steps closer her voice rising
do you see now colin
do you finally understand
i am not some guilty secret to be hidden
not just a body to sneak into when the door is shut
i am done with that
done with being quiet done with being careful

her fists clench at her sides
her bracelets clatter like chains snapping
i am not afraid of nobby anymore
let him rage let him break
i will not be his possession
i will not be the town's whisper
i am mine and i will take what i want

her eyes flare toward geralt
and do not think you can shame me either
copper or not
you stand here like judge and executioner
but i have lived long enough
in cages of men's judgment
this time i choose my own chains
or i choose none at all

her voice shakes the workshop walls
bold defiant reckless
her chest rising with every word
and colin stares wide eyed
his mouth dry his breath caught
watching a storm he cannot control
a fire he is too small to feed

her eyes
those blue eyes
holding the spark of everything still alive
wild fire under ash
the kind that refuses to die

her hair tumbled loose around her face
a curtain and a crown
and when she lifted her gaze
the whole shed shifted with her
even geralt felt it
that sharp current of will
that quiet unspoken message
i am not done
not yet
not ever

geralt does not flinch at her fury
he watches her blaze
then turns his gaze slow deliberate
back onto colin crumpled on the floor

his voice low steady
but each word a blade pressed close
you i will deal with
you are a thief a coward a boy
who steals from mates
and empties his balls for trouble
your kind i have seen a hundred times
and every one ended the same
broken forgotten buried

colin shakes   his lips moving
but no sound finds the air
sweat sliding down his neck
eyes darting for escape that does not exist

then geralt shifts
his shoulders softening his tone cooling
when he speaks to her it is different
not gentle not kind
but measured
as if she were fire he must not smother

i hear you
he says evenly
your anger your choice
you want a life that is yours
that is your right
but know this
the man you cling to is not strong enough
to carry you there

his words hang
cold steel pressed against colin's skin
warm steady weight laid at her feet
a line drawn in the dust between them

colin's chest rattles shallow
his breath a wheeze of panic
he claws at the floor as if the bolts and dust
might somehow anchor him
his voice spills out in fragments
please i did not mean it
i was only trying to make something of myself
i just wanted her
i just wanted a chance

tears blur his eyes streak his cheeks
he bows his head to the concrete
the smell of oil and rust filling his lungs
i will stop i swear i will stop
no more lies no more copies no more her
just do not tell nobby
please please

his words tumble fast tripping over each other
like a child begging forgiveness
like a thief caught red handed
with nothing left but shame
his shoulders shake
his whole body small
a trembling figure beneath the weight of steel and law
cowardice spilling from every pore

while geralt watches unmoved
and the woman beside him burns with fire
colin collapses deeper into dust
each sob another nail in the coffin of his pride

she steps forward once more
her voice slicing through colin's whimpers
enough she says again but this time harder
enough of your grovelling colin
enough of your threats geralt
i will not stand here watching men circle like dogs
deciding who owns me who punishes who forgives

her eyes burn bright her mouth set firm
i am not a prize to be fought over
not a secret to be hidden under dust and iron
i am not only nobby's wife
not your pity colin
not your judgment geralt
i am mine
do you hear me
mine

she rips at the torn blouse
lets it fall open bare skin daring the hot air
let the whole damn town see if they must
let them whisper their poison
i am tired of fear tired of silence
if there is a price then i will pay it
but i will pay it on my own terms

her words crack against the steel walls
louder than the grinding machines
louder than colin's sobs
a storm claiming its sky
a fire refusing to be smothered

geralt's jaw tightens but he does not move
the workshop hums with the echo of her words
for a long heartbeat there is only her breathing
colin's muffled sobs and the smell of rust

then geralt speaks
low and steady like gravel under boots
i am not here to own you
his eyes still on her
nor to drag you back to nobby
a man has no right to cage a woman
he says it flat
not as comfort but as fact

he shifts his weight
and the shadow falls across colin again
but this one
his boot nudges the trembling man on the floor
this one is a liar
a thief
a coward who will drag you down into the mud
he will not save you when the desert closes in
he will not stand beside you when fists rise
he will sell your name
like he sold harry's work

geralt straightens slow
his hands clasped behind his back
if you want a life that is yours
walk out of here on your feet
walk out clean
leave him here to face what he has made
leave him to the men he has cheated

his eyes flicker for just a moment
a glint of something softer
buried under the iron
then it is gone
and only the law of loyalty stands before them
hard and unmoving

chapter twenty eight

colin curls small in the dust
mewling words no one hears
his body slack with fear
his mouth too weak to shape courage
he is nothing now
less than the steel shavings
that litter the floor

geralt looks past him
only at her
his voice calm deliberate
you want out he says
then listen to me

when nobby heads to his claim tonight
the roads will be clear until dawn
pack light only what you can carry
take the southern track
not the main road
keep to the scrub until you reach a blue ute
there is a woman there
owes me a favour
she will hide you until the bus comes through

he pauses the weight of his words heavy
do not tell anyone
not your friends not your family
trust no one
quilpie bleeds its secrets into the ground
and men like nobby always hear them back
if you want freedom
you take it silent
you take it fast
and you do not look back

she swallows hard her eyes wide
but she does not flinch
his words are a map carved in stone
a way through the dust
a way out of the cage

colin groans at their feet
but neither of them looks down
his cowardice already written
his part already done

she breathes deep
the workshop air sharp with iron and oil
her torn blouse hanging loose
her hands trembling but her gaze steady

she nods once slow deliberate
i will do it she says
her voice low but clear
i will take the road i will take the chance
i will leave this town
leave the cage leave the whispers
i will not wait for nobby's fists
i will not die small in someone else's shadow

the weight of her words settles heavy
like steel laid true across the bench
she looks at geralt not colin
and what she sees in his eyes is not mercy
not softness
but a map a command a door unlatched

colin whines in the dust
but she does not turn to him
he has no place in her choice
his weakness lies crumpled on the concrete
and she is already beyond him

i will do it she repeats
and this time her voice is stronger
the sound of iron moving in the hot air
her decision forged
her rebellion set

night settles heavy across quilpie
cicadas screaming in the heat
the house thick with nobby's snores
each rise and fall of his chest a reminder
that time is thin and precious

nobby wakes
with the sun crouching behind the hills
his breath thick with the morning's beer
the air around him humming with flies
she has his meal ready
a plate of curling bacon
the edges crispy how he likes it
toast smoothed with butter
and a mug of tea a thermos filled for the night

nobby eats without words
scraping the enamel plate with his knife
the sound as piercing as the heat
then he wipes his mouth with the back of his hand
grunts his thanks or something like it
and heads for his claim
boots crunching over brown dirt
his shadow long and bent
the ute coughing into the distance
leaving her in the stillness
and the wide wide silence of her chance

breathing easier now but still nervous
as the silence settles around her shoulders
like a warning

her hands still tremble
but now it's not fear
it's fury that moves through her veins
slow and electric
like a storm waiting to break

she realises it's not him alone
not colin with his tears and need
nor nobby with his fists and threats
but the whole machine
that told her she was nothing
unless someone claimed her

she remembers the magazines
the glossy smiles
the whispered lessons
of how to please how to stay quiet
how to twist herself small
so men would feel large

she remembers the church pews
and the eyes that weighed her
the jokes at school and in the workplace
the way the world laughed
when a woman spoke too loud

and now she sees it
how every story she was fed
was a cage disguised as comfort
how every warning was a leash

she straightens her back
breathes deep into the ache
the bag heavy at her side
but her spirit lighter than ever

beneath the dying sun
she steps out
not as body to be owned
not as vessel for want
but as woman
whole and wild and unrepentant
her heartbeat the drum
of a freedom long denied
her shadow long and certain
on the road ahead

the sky bruises pale above the gibber flats
last light seeping over the horizon
heat continuing pressing in heavy
the air still full of flies and silence

she slips from the house
leaving behind the thin walls
leaving behind
the poverty ridden soil of her garden
her bag clutched tight to her side
her steps soft across the dust
then each crunch of gravel
a gunshot in her ears
but no door slams open
no voice calls her name

the street lies empty
only the rusted shells of cars
and the dry breath of the desert watching
she keeps her eyes forward
geralt's command echoing steady
do not falter do not look back

past foodworks with the shutters down
past the bottle shop littered with cans
past the gidgee scrub at the edge of town
her pulse keeps time with her stride
her body trembling but unbroken
each step a nail in the coffin of fear

by the time the moon lifts soft and bright
she is on the southern track
dust curling around her calves
the road stretching endless
and in the distance
the promise of the blue ute
waiting

she does not turn her head
not once
quilpie already falling away
like a name she has shed
like skin she will not wear again

colin wakes on the cool concrete
the stink of oil and rust in his nose
his jeans still open his body sore
the machines around him silent witnesses
to his shame

he sits up groggy
mouth dry eyes stinging
the echo of her voice still buzzing
the memory of geralt's contempt
burning deeper than any wound

he looks for her
but the workshop is empty
only dust motes drifting in the shafts of light
only the clatter
of a loose sheet of tin in the wind
she is gone
gone beyond him
and he knows it
panic rises sharp in his throat
what will he do now
harry will demand his designs back
nobby will smell betrayal
geralt already has his measure
and the woman who gave him fire
has slipped away without him

he staggers to his feet
heart hammering
mind spinning through lies and excuses
could he run
could he vanish down the same roads
or would the desert swallow him whole
before he made it
could he face nobby
face harry
face himself

he rubs his face with shaking hands
but no answer comes
only the truth
he is weak
he is small
and the world is closing in
steel walls pressing tighter each hour

the workshop once his kingdom
is now his cell
and colin knows it
knows the reckoning is coming
knows he cannot stop it

colin paces the workshop floor
boots scuffing through dust and filings
mind racing faster than his breath
schemes colliding half formed half rotten

he could run he tells himself
take the ute load it quick
head for the border
but where would he go
every town is smaller than it seems
every road carries whispers
and geralt's eyes would follow

he could grovel to nobby
spin some lie
say it was only once
say she came to him
but nobby is no fool
nobby would smell the fear
and break him in half
before the words dried in his mouth

he could claim the art as his
double down louder harder
push more copies online
sell before harry can prove him wrong
but even that fantasy crumbles

geralt knows
and now geralt knows
the whole world knows

colin's head throbs with the weight of it
hands pulling at his hair
sweat dripping into his eyes
there must be a way
some clever angle some trick
but every plan collapses into dust
every door closes before it opens
because he is too small too weak
to carry the lies he has made

he sinks onto the bench
heart pounding body shaking
scheming himself in circles
knowing deep down
there is no scheme left
only the reckoning waiting outside

colin strips off the stink of sweat and fear
the shower scalds his skin
steam filling the cracked tiles
he scrubs until he is red raw
as if water could wash away geralt's eyes
as if soap
could scrub clean the sound of her moans
or the taste of her rebellion

afterward he fries bacon
the fat spitting sharp in the pan
eggs bubbling yellow and rich
he eats fast greedy
mouth full grease dripping down his chin
fortified with food
stuffing courage into his gut
as if a full belly could armour his spine

he wipes his hands on a cloth
stands in the kitchen breathing deep
and tells himself out loud
i will survive
the words thin but he repeats them
again and again
until they almost sound true

back in the loungeroom he boots the computer
the old screen humming to life
facebook marketplace waiting
his photos ready
harry's designs dressed in his own false name
a lie for sale once more

his fingers shake on the keys
but he pushes through
upload after upload
rusted roses
stacked steel spheres
desert pea flowers reaching skyward
each one stamped with his fake pride

reckless but determined
the only way he knows
to keep moving
to keep breathing
to keep the world from closing in

the listings go live
colin leans back in his chair
the fan rattling overhead
sweat still drying on his neck
his belly heavy with bacon and eggs
his nerves raw but buzzing

for a long while nothing
just the empty hum of the computer
the silence of the workshop
the rusted pieces standing guard

then a ping
a message flashing bright on the screen
interested in the sturt desert pea
cash buyer passing through town
can we see it today

colin's heart leaps hard in his chest
his hands slam the desk
yes yes of course
he types fast desperate
his pulse racing with sudden fire

false hope swells in him thick
see he mutters *see i can make this work*
i am not finished
i am not weak
one sale one chance
this is survival
this is how i win

he imagines money in hand
diesel in his ute
second-hand steel in the yard
her body maybe even back in his arms
the future rewritten in a single click
he grins wide
eyes bright
blind
to the shadow
gathering just beyond the screen

the message had lit him up
and now colin waits at his own front door
nervous energy rolling in his gut
he has not cleaned a thing
but the thought of money in hand
makes him believe none of it matters

the shack squats low in the heat
asbestos sheets weathered grey
edges curling sharp and brittle
grubby curtains sag in the windows
yellowed lace once white
now stained with years of dust and smoke
inside the air is stale
thick with sweat and rust
the floor a patch of dirty brown carpet
threadbare and clotted with grit
who in their right mind lays carpet in the desert
he wonders for the hundredth time
each step raising a faint puff of brown dust
that never leaves
no matter how much you beat it

metal copies lean against every wall
roses rusted at the edges
flowers bent out of symmetry
spheres piled clumsy in the corner
another sturt desert pea looming half-polished
its shine dulled by fingerprints and lies
his house is no gallery
but a graveyard of stolen designs

the knock comes
three sharp raps
against the wooden door
colin jumps
runs a hand through his sweaty hair
wipes sweat on his jeans
and pulls it open wide

the buyer steps across the threshold
his boots sinking into the filthy carpet
dust rising in little clouds with every step
he does not comment
just lets his eyes roam slow
taking in the shack's sagging ceilings
the piles of bent steel
the half-finished roses and crooked spheres

colin follows close eager
gesturing with wide hands
this one sold well online
and here see the detail
look at the weld there
takes a steady hand that does
his voice quick full of false pride
every word a rehearsed lie
but the buyer only nods
quiet calm eyes sharp behind the mask

he kneels at the sturt desert pea
runs his fingers along the mesh
feels the rough edges where colin's welds waver
murmurs *impressive work*
though his mouth curves almost too smooth
as if the words cost him nothing

colin chatters on
trying to fill the silence
offering prices
offering delivery
offering more pieces at discount
his voice cracking but still trying
as if sound itself could prove his worth

the buyer drifts from corner to corner
examining the copies without urgency
each pause another nail in colin's coffin
each nod another silent judgment
he says little
but his eyes say everything
they are not the eyes of a customer
they are the eyes of a man taking measure
the eyes of someone reporting back

colin cannot see it
too blinded by hunger
too deafened by hope
he only smiles wider
believing the sale already his

colin rubs his palms together
pacing behind the buyer like a dog at heel
his grin wide his eyes fevered
he cannot stop the words tumbling out

see how clean that line is
took me days to get it right
and no one else in quilpie can match it
people will pay top dollar for work like this
they already do online
got interest
from as far as brisbane last month
he adds the lie quick
hoping it will stick like fresh weld

the buyer hums low
runs a hand over a metal rose
turns it in the light as though it were fine
colin watches hungry
reads silence as agreement
reads every nod as approval

he wipes sweat from his brow
imagines cash counted into his hands
imagines a ute full of diesel
imagines beers at the saltbush café
people slapping his back calling him artist
imagines her slipping back into his arms
now that he can provide
now that he can prove himself
more than nobby
more than harry
more than anyone ever gave him credit for

he feels tall again
strong again
the bacon and eggs in his gut
swelling into courage
his fear of geralt fading
his shame at her words dissolving
this is my turning point he whispers inside
this is how i win back my life

he does not see
the way the buyer's eyes flick cold
he does not hear the quiet note of calculation
he only hears the clink of imagined coins
he only feels the glow of false triumph
and he convinces himself
the deal is already his

the buyer finally speaks his name
schultsy he says deep voice calm
dark grey curly hair clean shaven
thick arms folded pretty fit
his smile no longer faint
now it carries weight
something colin cannot read
colin beams back desperate
good to meet you mate good to meet you
you will not regret this piece i swear
one of my best
he pats the metal desert pea
as if the touch alone makes it true
schultsy glances once toward the door
and there he is

geralt chadowski
boots heavy against the carpeted floor
hat low shadowing eyes that gleam like iron
not the law not tonight
only justice shaped in his own image
colin's grin falters lips dry
his eyes dart between them
the buyer and the sergeant
the clean shaven stranger with measuring eyes
and the copper who has no warrant no file
only the cold fire of his own mission

what is this colin croaks
his voice thin his throat tight
you said you wanted the piece
you said you would pay cash

schultsy's lips twitch with a humourless smile
i said i was interested
and i was
interested to see just how much of a fool you are

geralt steps closer
the shack closing in with him
his voice steady
you thought you were clever colin
stealing harry's welds
selling lies for coin
you thought lust would carry you
thought hunger would make you a man

his shadow falls across the carpet
dust rising like smoke at his feet
but there is no badge in his hand
no book of charges
only contempt
only the weight of his own justice

colin's chest caves
the bacon and eggs now stones in his gut
the sweat dripping cold down his back
his false hope shrivels in the silence
as the truth lands heavy
he has no buyer
he has no woman
he has no escape

only geralt
only schultsy
and the rusted evidence of every lie
piled around him like a grave

geralt steps forward slow deliberate
the asbestos walls shiver with each boot fall
his hands loose at his sides
but the weight of him heavier than any weapon

you are looking for the law colin
geralt says voice low steady
but the law does not live here
not in quilpie not in these shacks
out here there is only honour
and you do not have any his eyes sweep the room
the bent roses the crooked spheres
the sturt desert pea half polished half fraud
this is not art
this is theft hammered into steel
you sold harry's sweat as your own
you spat on the trust of mates
and for what
a few notes in your pocket
a few fucks in the dark

schultsy leans on the doorframe
arms crossed
his dark grey curly hair catching the light
silent but solid as a wall
and colin knows he cannot run through him

geralt's gaze cuts back sharp
i am not here with papers
i am not here with warrants
i am here because a man like you
poisons the ground he walks on
and the desert has a way of cleaning itself

he bends close until his eyes meet colin's
his breath hot with dust and certainty
you have two choices boy
you face nobby
or you face me

the words settle thick as iron filings
colin's mouth works useless
his body trembling small
because he knows either way
there is no law to save him
only justice waiting with bare hands

geralt's fists want blood
but his jaw stays tight
he has worn the uniform too long
lived too many years keeping rage chained
discipline hammered into his bones
justice yes but never vengeance

he straightens slow deliberate
his voice calm now almost quiet
be the man you want to be colin
not the coward on this floor
not the thief hiding behind stolen welds
not the boy crying for mercy in his own shack
stand up
choose what kind of man you will walk out as
because in the end no one else can do it for you

the words hang in the stale air
he turns his back without hurry
schultsy uncrosses his arms
gives colin one long unreadable look
and follows geralt through the wooden door

the shack is silent again
the dust drifting in the light
the bent roses leaning in the corners
the carpet holding the stink of years

colin alone
his chest hollow his breath shallow
geralt's words still burning
be the man you want to be

and yet he cannot move
cannot rise
because he does not know what kind of man that is
or if there is any man left in him at all

the road ahead shivers with heat ghosts
the woman in the blue ute drives on
jaw set eyes hard against the dark
each rise and dip a gamble with what moves unseen
kangaroos burst from the scrub
thudding past in the wash of light
the air thick with dust and fear
and the taste of leaving

the passenger clutches her bag close
rings cold against her skin
she feels the weight of silence
how it presses heavier than any word
she wonders if this woman knows her story
if geralt told her of nobby
of nights that burned too long
of the promise made and the price of it

the driver does not turn her head
the wheel steady in her hands
her gaze fixed on the narrow strip ahead
each kilometre a quiet defiance
she has driven others before
women with hollow eyes and trembling hands
she knows not to ask
not to look too long

the stars hang low over the plains
wide and white and watching
the road a thin thread through the dark
neither speaks as the hours fold in
the hum of the tyres becomes a prayer
to reach the bus before dawn
to keep moving
to keep breathing
to survive the night

in her mind quilpie is already fading
the shacks sagging in the hot sunlight
the bottle shop the post office
the squat houses buried in dust
she does not turn her head
does not glance back
geralt's voice steady in her ear
do not falter do not look back

her breath is tight in her chest
fear and freedom tangled in each inhale
her stomach knots with what she has left behind
nobby's shadow
colin's weakness
the town's whispers thick as flies

but her hands are steady in her lap
her jaw firm
every kilometre
another thread snapping loose
every bend in the road
another weight discarded
the desert night opening wide before her
empty and endless
but also hers

she leans her forehead to the window glass
as slowly the morning sun creeps across her skin
she whispers low to herself
i am mine now
mine

the bus wheezes to a stop at the station
heat shimmers off the tin roof
and there she is   sue
broad shouldered tight jeans riding boots
eyes sharp as a hawk yet kind beneath the brim

you must be her she says low
not a question but a certainty
come inside quick now
before anyone sees

the woman follows through the side door
into a back room cool and dim
the smell of bread and soap thick in the air
sue sets down the bag on a wooden chair
pours her a glass of water
watching close as she drinks

you are not the first sue says
her voice calm steady as stone
and you will not be the last
this country eats its women
spits them out silent
but there is a way through if you are willing
a road not marked on any map

sue leans in whispers names
places hidden safehouses
scattered through the scrub
women who know how to move unseen
men who drive road trains
and do not ask questions
a network stitched together
quiet threads of resistance
winding across australia

drink your water sue says
rest here till tomorrow's ride
then you will go on further
you keep your head down
you trust the hands that take you in
and you remember always
you are not his anymore
you are your own

the woman swallows hard
her heart pounding not with fear
but with something new
something like hope

the shack is hot thick with flies
colin slumped in a chair staring at the floor
the carpet dark with old stains
the air stale with rust and grease

he has not eaten since the bacon and eggs
his stomach knots sour
his hands twitch restless on his knees
he cannot shake geralt's words
be the man you want to be
but every time he repeats them
they collapse into dust

then the whispers begin
first at the bottle shop
then at foodworks
then carried on the miners' tongues in the pub
nobby's wife gone
no one saw her leave
no one knows where she went
but everyone is talking

colin hears it on the wind
the mutters drifting into his shack
the knowing looks when he walks the street
eyes cutting sharp through him
men shaking their heads
women turning away

he feels the ground tilt beneath him
his false sale forgotten
his fakes leaning heavy in the corners
every piece of steel a reminder
of what he stole what he lost
what he will never be

she is gone
truly gone
and the town knows it
knows he is part of it
though no one says his name yet
he can feel it gathering
like a dust storm on the horizon

colin crumbles further into himself
alone in the asbestos shell
surrounded by lies and silence
waiting for the storm to break

nobby storms through the pub door
eyes red from drink
fists clenched like stone
the miners fall silent one by one
their singlets stained with dust and sweat
their pint glasses frozen midair
because they all know what comes
when nobby's temper breaks

she is gone he roars
his voice rattling glasses on the shelves
gone like smoke
and none of you bastards saw a thing
his boots stamp the floor hard
his chest heaving like a bellows
spit flying from his mouth
mine he snarls *mine she was mine*
the room bends under his fury
men glance down at their beer
women slip out through the side door
no one dares step in front of him
until geralt does

geralt stands steady calm
arms loose at his sides
eyes like steel cutting through the heat
she was never yours nobby
he says low but the words carry
you did not own her
you never did
nobby's head jerks his jaw tight
what did you say
his fists rising ready to smash
but geralt does not move
he lets the silence crack between them
then repeats slow deliberate
she is not your possession
she is a woman not cattle
not opal not stone
not yours to drink or beat or keep

the miners shift uneasy
their weight shifting on boots
their eyes darting from nobby's fury
to geralt's calm
two kinds of power colliding in the stale beer air
nobby shakes his head
his mouth twisting
but for the first time
a flicker of doubt cracks the rage
because the words hang heavy
truer than the fists he wants to throw

nobby lunges fists swinging wild
a roar tearing from his throat
the pub air thick with sweat and fury
glasses topple chairs scrape
men scatter back to the walls
geralt does not flinch
he sidesteps sharp boots planted solid
lets nobby's punch cut only air
his hand lifts calm firm
pushing the miner's chest back without violence
without rage
controlled as stone

enough geralt says
voice steady over the chaos
you will not hit me
you will not hit anyone else
not for this
not for her
nobby growls fists raised again
but already the miners are shifting
already their whispers rising low
he lost her fair and square one mutters
she is no man's property
another shakes his head
been saying it for years
she deserved better than to rot in that shack

the murmurs swell like a tide
the words crawling into nobby's ears
dulling his fury with the sting of shame
his face red his breath ragged
his fists still tight
but his stance falters just enough
the weight of the room tilting against him

geralt's eyes do not leave his
you hear them
you hear the truth
she walked away because she chose to
and no amount of your fists
will drag her back

the miners nod muttering louder
their loyalty to nobby thinning
their silence cracking open at last
and for the first time
nobby stands not as king of the pub
but as a man alone in his rage

nobby's fists still twitch but the tide is gone
the miners' eyes turned sharp
their murmurs cutting deeper than blows
he spits on the floor snarls low
fuck the lot of you
and storms out into the night
boots pounding on the pub boards
his shadow swallowed by dust and heat
his power broken in the space of a breath

the pub exhales as one
men shake their heads
women whisper low
the silence cracked forever
nobby no longer untouchable
no longer the law of his own house

and across town in his asbestos shack
colin hears it
the whispers carried faster than the wind
she is gone
nobby lost his grip
geralt stood against him and did not flinch
the miners turning their backs
the balance shifting

colin sits in his chair
dirty carpet under his feet
metal copies leaning in the corners
and feels the world tilting
the cage rattling apart around them all
his fear curling tighter
his false hope shrivelling thin
because if nobby can be broken
if she can walk away
then what is left for him
a thief a coward a hollow man
waiting for the desert to decide his fate

nobby stomps into the dark
the desert night heavy with heat and silence
his breath sharp his fists aching empty
the pub's murmurs still ringing in his ears
she walked away they said
she is no man's property they dared
their words burned hotter than the grog in his veins

he kicks a rusted drum sends it rolling
curses spit from his mouth like sparks
he will not be made a fool
not by her not by geralt
not by a town of weak men whispering in corners
his rage swells dark and aimless
searching for a throat to close his hands around
searching for a way to take back what he lost

while across town colin sits hunched
in his asbestos shack
the walls closing tighter each hour
the carpet stinking hot beneath his feet
he hears the echoes carried fast on the wind
nobby shamed in the pub
geralt steady unbroken
the miners murmuring loud enough for all to hear

paranoia gnaws at him sharp
if nobby comes he will kill him
if geralt comes he will break him
if the town comes they will spit on him
and in every shadow colin sees their eyes
in every creak of the shack he hears their boots
he cannot eat
he cannot sleep
he paces the filthy floor
hands shaking lips muttering
i can survive i can survive
but the words ring hollow in the stale air

nobby's rage out in the dust
colin's fear in the shack's rotten walls
two men circling the same void
both bound by the woman who walked away
both undone
by what they thought they owned

geralt moves through quilpie at his own pace
boots striking the brown dust
with measured weight
he has seen men break themselves on rage
seen others rot in fear
two sides of the same coin
and now he watches both spin in the hot air

nobby stomps the outskirts
his curses rolling across the flats
his fists empty his pride bleeding
he is a storm without lightning
all noise and shadow
and geralt lets him rage
lets him wear himself thin against the night

colin curls inside his shack
eyes wild in the half dark
every creak a threat every knock a noose
he mutters plans that melt
as quick as they form
sweat slick on his skin
the stink of grease and rust thick around him
and geralt knows the man is already undone
he does not need a fist
only time

geralt stands at the crossroads of their ruin
watchful silent
not as the law not tonight
but as something older
a witness a weight
a reminder that choices carve men open
and that no one can save them
from themselves

he keeps his temper in check
he always does
because justice here is not about punishment
but about stripping men bare
until only truth is left
and truth is heavier than iron
truth is what neither nobby nor colin can carry

the bus rattles deeper into the scrub
each mile putting quilpie even further behind
each mile stripping the dust of that life
from her skin
the heat still presses heavy
but it no longer feels like a cage
it feels like space

sue's promise carries her forward
her whispers
of safe houses scattered through the country
women who open their doors without questions
men who drive road trains
but keep their mouths shut
a web of quiet resistance
stitched into the land
holding her now like unseen arms

she sips water from a dented flask
her fingers tight around it
her rings
catching light through the cracked window
she thinks of nobby's fists
of colin's weakness
of geralt's iron words
and she feels the knot in her chest
slowly unwind

the other passengers keep their eyes to themselves
a silent courtesy in outback travel
but one woman across the aisle
gives the faintest nod
and she feels it deep
that small recognition
a sign she is not alone

the bus hums steady
the road stretches endless
and for the first time in years
she breathes
without the weight of someone else's name
she whispers again to herself
i am mine
and the words no longer tremble
they land sure
like steel cooling hard in the sun

the bus hisses to a stop at a siding town
little more than a fuel pump a faded motel sign
and a weatherboard hall with peeling paint
the driver calls out the name flat
but to her it sounds like a door swinging open

sue's words echo steady in her ear
ask for margaret
she will know what to do

the hall smells of eucalyptus and dust
inside women move quietly
sorting boxes of clothes tins of food
their eyes lift when she enters
not suspicious only watchful
measuring
whether she is ready to stand on her own
a tall woman with silver plaited hair
steps forward hand outstretched
you must be her she says
sue rang ahead
you'll be safe here for the night

the woman grips her hand firm
her heart beating fast but not from fear
from the sudden truth of it
a chain of hands reaching for her
a road laid out unseen
women helping each other through the cracks

margaret shows her a small room
bare bed clean sheet jug of water
you rest she says
tomorrow someone else will take you further
each step a little freer
each step further from the cage

she sits on the bed
sets her bag at her feet
and breathes deep for the first time
not as nobby's wife
not as colin's secret
only herself
alive inside her own name

night settles soft around the hall
the hum of crickets rising outside
the sheet cool beneath her back
for the first time in years she sleeps
without waiting for footsteps in the dark
without fearing the slam of a door

when she wakes the air smells of toast
laughter drifts faint through the thin walls
laughter not sharp or cruel
but easy
she stands in the doorway watching
margaret pouring tea
two younger women folding donated clothes
their chatter low steady
ordinary
and it feels like a miracle

she eats toast slowly
each bite a promise
her shoulders ease her breath lengthens
for the first time she lets herself wonder
what comes after running

she sees a small cottage in her mind
not grand
just walls that are hers
a window looking onto trees not dust
her rings glinting as she works with her hands
maybe clay maybe books
maybe even chooks
maybe nothing but quiet

she imagines waking each day
without a name tied to her wrist
without fear clamped to her chest
free to choose
free to change

the thought startles her
not because it is impossible
but because it feels close now
closer than ever before
a life that belongs only to her

the morning sun spills gold
across the little town
heat already rising from the gravel
but her chest feels lighter
her bag slung over her shoulder
her steps steady on the ground

margaret walks her to the back door of the hall
where a dusty white ute waits
a woman at the wheel tips her hat
brown skin weathered eyes kind
no questions asked
just space made on the bench seat

this is jo margaret says
she will take you to the next stop
you keep your head down
you keep moving
her hand squeezes tight around hers
not farewell but promise
that the chain will hold

the ute rattles onto the open road
the desert stretching wide and merciless
yet no longer a trap
each mile another thread cut free
each mile another choice waiting ahead

jo drives in silence for a while
then offers a bottle of water
and the faintest smile
we have all been where you are
different names same story
you're not alone out here

the words sink deep
stronger than any law
a quiet network stronger than dust and fists
a road built on whispers
and women refusing to vanish

she watches the horizon
red earth shifting into sky
and feels it again
the strange new pulse of hope
not only escape
but the first taste of belonging
in a life that is hers alone

the ute hums steady over rutted tracks
dust swirling behind them like ghosts
but she no longer feels chased
she feels carried

they stop at a roadside camp
tarps stretched against the sun
pots simmering over coals
children running barefoot in the red dirt
women tending them with easy voices
the sight catches in her chest
so ordinary so alive

jo nods toward a bench beneath a tree
sit rest eat

she obeys slowly
the shade cool on her skin
a plate pressed into her hands
warm damper thick with butter
the taste simple and rich
like something she had forgotten
belonged to her

she watches the women laugh together
their heads bent close
their bracelets jangling
their voices sure
and for the first time she sees herself
not as a fugitive
not as a possession
not as a secret lover
but as a woman among women
a thread in a larger weave

her hands no longer tremble
her shoulders square
she touches the rings on her fingers
not as shackles
but as reminders that she shines still
that she has always shone
only now she is free to see it

she whispers
her own name under her breath
slow careful
as though she is meeting herself again
and when she hears it
she smiles
because it sounds strong
because it sounds true

night settles at the roadside camp
the sky a wide bowl of stars
the fire crackles low
voices fade into murmurs and quiet laughter
children curled in blankets
the desert holding its breath

she sits apart for a moment
watching the flames
her bag at her feet light now
because the weight she carried
was never in the cloth or the clothes
it was in the silence she lived under
and that silence has broken

jo sits beside her
passing a ceramic mug of tea
no words just presence
steam rising into the cool air
the woman sips slow
the warmth running through her chest
her shoulders unknotted
her breath steady

for the first time
she lets herself imagine
not only escape but future
a cottage with a small verandah
a garden waiting for her to work in
hands dirty from planting not from scrubbing
friends around her who know her name
and say it without tying it to any man
she imagines learning again
books open in her lap
paper covered in her own words
teaching children to read perhaps
or teaching herself a new craft
something that belongs only to her
woven fibres woven words
woven life

her rings glint in the firelight
not as chains now
but as proof that she can adorn herself
because she chooses to
because she deserves to

she whispers once more
i am mine
but now the words stretch further
not only claim
but promise
to build to grow to live

morning comes with pale light across the camp
the desert cool for a brief hour
before the sun burns it dry again
she wakes early
helps stoke the fire with dry sticks
her hands moving steady
not from habit but from choice
she pours water into a pot
listens to it hiss and settle
a small act yet her own

jo nods approving
handing her a loaf of damper to slice
you will find your place she says
we all do
words simple but weighted
like stone set at the base of a new wall

after breakfast she asks for paper
one of the women
pulls a crumpled pad from a biscuit tin
and a stub of pencil
she takes it with care
her fingers trembling slightly
then steadies herself
and begins to write her name
again and again across the page

not his name
not borrowed not bound
only hers
each letter stronger than the last
until the page is covered
until she feels it in her bones

later she helps mend a tarp
threading twine through canvas
the needle pulling clean
her hands learning new work
the kind that builds rather than hides
each stitch a step
each knot a claim

when the sun climbs high
and sweat slicks her back
she stands tall in the shade
looks at the camp bustling
and for the first time thinks
this is living
this is real
and she is part of it

days pass measured by the rising and falling sun
the camp hums with small tasks
voices lifted low in rhythm with work
and she begins to move among them
not as guest not as stranger
but as thread drawn into fabric
she carries water from the tank
dust clinging to her calves
laughing with a young girl who splashes her hands
she kneads flour into dough
her bracelets rattling soft like music
she sits in the evening circle
listening to stories of other women who came
women who stayed
women who moved further down the line
each tale a map of survival
each face proof she is not alone

at first she is quiet
the weight of years pressing her tongue
but little by little words come
her voice sliding into the stream
a story told here
a question asked there
until her laughter joins theirs
unforced unhidden
bright as a bell in the dry night air

she learns to sew patches onto worn shirts
her fingers pricked but steady
she helps grind ochre for paint
watching colours bloom in her palm
red and yellow streaking her skin
as if reminding her of blood and sun
as if saying you belong to the earth
before you belong to any man

each day she feels her name grow louder
not whispered not stolen
but spoken clear by her own lips
and heard by others who nod in return
recognising her not as possession
not as secret
but as woman whole and alive

and in the quiet of the fire
she touches her rings
and no longer wonders if she deserves to wear them
she knows she does
because she shines
because she has always shone

the days blur into rhythm
chores and stories
shared meals and quiet evenings
the work hard but steady
the kind that fills the body with tiredness
not dread

she learns to bake damper without burning it
her hands dusted white with flour
she helps string beads for children's necklaces
colours flashing bright in the sun
she listens to the women laugh
their voices strong not brittle
their joy unhidden
and for the first time she feels herself
not on the edge of life
but in the centre of it

when margaret visits again
she greets her not as rescuer
but as equal
sits shoulder to shoulder over cups of tea
and tells her plainly
i am not running anymore
i am living
and the words feel strange on her tongue
strange but true

she begins to speak of what comes next
of work she might do
of places she might go
of a cottage she imagines still
walls painted white
a small garden of herbs
space for other women to come
to sit to rest to breathe free

her voice steadies with each telling
her dream hardening into plan
a map traced not in fear
but in hope
each detail
hammering new strength into her spine
each step a piece of ground claimed

at night she lies beneath the wide sky
stars endless above her
and instead of thinking of escape
she thinks of tomorrow
of what she can build
and for the first time in years
her body feels her own
her future her own
her name her own

chapter fifty nine

she wakes before dawn
the camp still wrapped in shadow
and walks to the edge where the desert opens wide
the horizon pale with coming light
her breath even her chest calm
she no longer feels hunted
she feels rooted

when she returns
jo hands her a small notebook
pages clean ready
for plans not secrets
write it down jo says
so it cannot slip away
so you can see it take shape

and she does
each page filled with the bones of a new life
a place with whitewashed walls
herbs growing in reclaimed pots
a table where women can sit and rest
a kettle always on the boil
a door that opens without fear

margaret brings names
contacts who will help her find work
a cousin who can spare timber
a sister with tools
an auntie with seeds
threads drawn together into something strong
a net not to trap but to hold
to keep her steady as she builds
she learns more each day
to patch clothes with neat stitches
to knead dough with sure hands
to speak without apology
her voice carrying like smoke across the fire
and each task is no longer survival
it is foundation
each act laying down stone
for the life she is claiming
at night she touches her rings
feels their cool weight   and smiles
they are no longer reminders of possession
they are promises
that she will always adorn herself
that she will always shine
she is not running now
she is moving forward
her name carved clear
her vision alive
the woman she is
woven into her own story at last

she was once a shadow in another man's house
her name swallowed her body caged
her laughter pressed down into silence

but she walked away
through dust through danger
through whispers sharp as knives
she stepped into her own name
and claimed it like flame

she found hands that lifted not held
voices that wove her into belonging
a network of women
like roots beneath desert soil
invisible but unbreakable
their strength carrying her forward

she learned to mend to knead to speak
to write her name without trembling
to dream not as escape but as foundation
walls painted white
a garden small but alive
a door opening wide to whoever needs it

now she stands unchained
her rings gleaming as promises
not of ownership but of choice
her body her voice her future her own

she is no man's possession
she is not silence
she is not shadow
she is her own light
and she shines without apology

reflecting

who looks out for the women who vanish
first nations sisters whose names are spoken
only by family and wind
police reports thin as dust
searches that end before they begin
their faces on fences
their spirits still waiting beside the road

when a woman says she must leave
listen
do not ask for proof
do not measure her fear against your comfort
her story does not need your permission
it needs your protection
it needs your belief

she knows she cannot save them all
but she can bear witness
she can light candles at windows
learn their stories speak their names
stand beside the mothers who wait
and whisper to the wind
i am watching

safety is not a wall
it is a circle
drawn by women who refuse to forget
linked by hands unseen but unbroken
their strength carried through generations
their love the oldest law
their fire the light that guides the lost

reckoning

nobby called it love but meant possession
his hands the law his house the cage
he believed her breath belonged to him
that her silence was consent
that her leaving was betrayal not survival

colin shaped her body from steel
as if the curve of her hip might forgive him
as if beauty could erase what he took
but the metal never softened
and in its reflection he saw himself
not artist not saviour
just another man mistaking want for worth

geralt saw all of it
the rot beneath the red dust
he knew
the law could not hold what needed healing
so he stood back let her walk free
knowing sometimes salvation
is distance not deliverance

and what then of the future
when so many women must vanish to live
when leaving is the only safety offered
when first nations sisters
still disappear into silence
and the news scrolls on as if nothing happened

still she walks
head high through the burning plain
carrying the weight of every woman still waiting
she is the proof that freedom costs too much
and the promise that one day   it will not
we are the ones who walked away
who ran through dust and fire
who left behind men who called it love
and meant control
we are the ones who buried silence
and planted truth in its place
we do not wait for rescue
we build it
with each other's hands
we weave safety from story
courage from care
our daughters will not need to vanish to be free
the future begins in the voices that rise
from kitchen tables and courtrooms
from country and city alike
we speak the names of the missing
we demand their return
we claim the earth beneath our feet
as the place of our belonging
not his not theirs
ours
and when we lift our faces to the wide australian sky
we see not the ache of what was lost
but the fierce unbroken light
of women who remain
and who will not
ever again
bow

"Art is not a frill on the frock of life, it is the very fabric: without it we are naked to the often cruel, harsh and unjust elements of life."

Archer, Robyn. Detritus: Addressing Culture & the Arts. UWA Publishing, 2010. (Publisher page quoting the line).

Nelson, Alice. "Archer hits the mark." The West Australian, 12 Aug 2010. (Discusses Robyn Archer's "frill/fringe on the frock of life" motif.)

"Art is not a frill on the frock of life, but the very fabric with which it is woven" Robyn Archer AO
Singer and Artistic Director
This tile embedded on the path surrounding Hamer Hall at the Arts Centre Melbourne 25 June 2022

"Art is not a frill on the frock of life, it is the very fabric: without it we are naked to the often cruel, harsh and unjust elements of life."
Mosaic embedded into the foundations of a Nuriootpa house.
Facebook Rhagodia Mosaics and Collage
2014 August 20
2014 December 1
2019 January 1
2020 January 1

to the campfire readers who were with me all the way
while writing *desert deluge* where harry was conceived
then harry appears as a minor character in *river refuge*
then *desert centrifuge* and *river subterfuge*

to shirley sheila and pat the aunties whose voices echo
through the shed biscuits tea and truth woven into every
spark

to geralt whose laughter shakes the walls and morgan
whose sharp eyes keep the fire honest

to alex who widened the road who showed that networks
can be welded too

to robyn archer ao whose words have held me steady for
many years
*"Art is not a frill on the frock of life, it is the very fabric:
without it we are naked to the often cruel, harsh and unjust
elements of life."*

to the readers of *desert deluge* who asked for more sex
who asked where the heat was whose questions sparked
these verses

to all who know that sex is not shame and art is not extra
but both are survival both are pride both are love

to robyne lesley as first reader whose feedback focused
not on the sex but on the support and kindness shown to
the woman travelling alone

to destroy the joint who started a movement to unite us
all to stop hate speech, sexism and bigotry
https://catalogue.nla.gov.au/catalog/6180423
destroy the joint (DJT) aims to track how many women
die each year due to violence
the group uses its platform to build an online community
for those concerned with violence towards women
#destroythejoint

to jena and sabrina who brainstormed with me for an arts
project that acknowledged dead women

to robyne whose zonta adelaide torrens networks
ensured the exhibition of the five panels which paid
homage to the women murdered in australia between
2019 and 2023
https://heathergordon.com.au/spaces-and-
places/sala/respect-the-women-sala-2024/

to chado who showed me the arid zone landscape around
andamooka in slow survey from the reef green xg falcon
ute

and to ben for the conversations about the usefulness of
shed beers for thinking

for the real women
margaret sue and jo
who hold space for others
through storm and stillness
who acknowledge the courage it takes
to leave what harms
to build again from quiet beginnings

for the women across the long roads
and red horizons of rural and remote australia
where refuges for women are few
and help can feel far away
where silence is mistaken for strength
and old beliefs
still whisper that pain is private
that a woman must endure
that love is measured in what she forgives

for those who have been told
it is their fault
for the men who were taught
that violence is manhood
for the sons growing up
searching for another way
and the daughters learning
that tenderness is power

for those who do not look away
who open doors in darkness
who lend a car or a couch or a kind word
who say *no more*
and mean it with their whole heart

this is for you
the quiet builders of safety and truth
the ones who keep compassion alive
in places where it is needed most
your courage is the forge
where new stories are shaped
and where love
at last
holds its own weight in the fire

https://www.respect.gov.au/support-services

1800 737 732

Australia